THE RADICAL VIEW

SCREENPLAY AND INTRODUCTION BY

GREGORY LeGRAND KERNS

Published by G. LeGrand Publishing 2008
Visit www.GLeGrand.com

THE RADICAL VIEW SCREENPLAY AND INTRODUCTION
BY GREGORY LEGRAND KERNS

ISBN: 978-0-615-21529-7

Published by G. LeGrand Publishing

Cover designed by Gregory LeGrand Kerns

**For more information about the writer,
visit www.GregoryLeGrandKerns.com**

Thanks to J.D. Roth for giving me my first big break.

Special thanks to Jeff Menell for helping me
mind my grammatical Ps and Qs.

Extra special thanks to my late mother Sallie B. Kerns
for telling me to never stop writing.

CONTENTS

INTRODUCTION

BY GREGORY LEGRAND KERNS

Warning. This film has not yet been produced. You won't find it coming soon to a theater near you—at least not at the time of this writing. And you won't find glossy photos of big name movie stars. Not here. But what you will find is the exclusive opportunity to experience *The Radical View* before it's made into a movie. Before Hollywood messes it up.

I'll bet you're thinking, "What's so special about this unproduced screenplay?" It's special because this 100-plus page document changed my life. This script launched my writing career. It wasn't the first screenplay I wrote. In fact, it was number seven or eight. Trust me, you don't want to read those earlier screenplays. While living in Atlanta and working at Houston's Restaurants, I wrote and shipped several scripts to LA only to have them return with rejection letters. I still have copies of the scripts and the rejection letters. I tried to recycle the paper by printing on the blank side, but even my printer rejected the pages. Still, I didn't give up. I continued to work hard at perfecting my craft. Thanks to *The Radical View*, I've been a gainfully employed writer for more than a decade now. Numerous high-profile companies have hired me as a writer. More about that later.

The Beginning

Flashback to 1991. Grunge music is growing. MC Hammer is sizzling. Vanilla Ice is melting. That's when I peeled out of the Peach State and headed for the Golden State in my loaded-down, beat-up Volkswagen Golf. I drove cross country with no air conditioning, no Triple-A card and no cell phone (back then, only three people in the world owned mobile phones). Good thing it didn't rain because I barely had windshield wipers. And

When I arrived in California, I was sporting a Billy Dee Williams-style hairdo. Hey, at least it wasn't a Jheri curl.

it's not because I think windshield wipers are evil. I simply could not afford new ones. I only started to sweat when I was about to run out of gas in the middle of the desert. To make matters worse, every road sign said, "Do not pick up hitchhikers, Arizona State Prison." All the while, my gas needle was dropping faster than Milli Vanilli's record sales after their lip sync debacle. When I finally found a station, I didn't care that gas was five bucks a gallon. Shortly after I arrived in Cali, I sat down and wrote *The Radical View*. My objective was to sell the script so I could retire from the restaurant business.

The Response

No sale. *The Radical View* never sold, but it opened a lot of doors for me. First, it helped me land a manager, Geoffrey H. Miller. From day one, Geoff believed in the script wholeheartedly. Thank you, Charles Allen, for introducing us. Not only did Geoff and I work closely on developing the script, we also co-founded the company Unique Tree Films. After nearly a decade of collaborating on various film projects, including producing the independent feature *The Good-Bye Tape*, we dissolved the business. Today we are still close personal friends. He was a groomsman in my wedding.

Second, the script's strength helped us get meetings at virtually every movie studio and major production company in Tinseltown. Literary agents, studio executives and film producers would read the script and call us in for a meeting. Geoff and I were thrilled. It was like magic, I tell ya. I thought it would always be this easy. Who knew?

The Staged Reading

Can you say, "Free lunch"? Because the script was getting such great response, Geoff decided to use his savings to produce a staged reading on the Universal Studios lot. The production was a huge success. The industry-filled audience hung on every word spoken by our amazingly talented cast. Anne Nyberg was captivating in the role of Ashley, Michael Anthony Rawlins played the part of Brandon to the hilt and Charles Allen kept the audience rolling in the aisles with his comedic performance of Peanut. In addition to providing much needed emotional support during rehearsal, Regina Ryer, my roommate at the time, delivered a kick-butt performance in the role of Mary. Not only did the reading help us get more meetings, but it also helped us get a few free meals. Not at the Ivy or Spago. More like the studio commissary. But still, it was a free lunch.

The Aftermath

Connections. Based on the ones made from *The Radical View*, I was able to land a paying job writing for television and join the Writers Guild of America—the ultimate validation for professional writers. And it didn't stop there. With writing credits on my resume from the Disney Channel, MTV and BET, I've had no problem landing other writing jobs, especially in advertising. Currently, I am an associate creative director in New York City with a handsome salary at one of the world's top advertising agencies. I still write and produce independent film projects in my free time.

The Radical View has given me the opportunity to write for legends like Dick Clark and Russell Simmons. And for all you

Def Comedy Jam fans who are wondering, Russell Simmons does know how to say more than, "Thank you for coming and have a good night." What's more, I've had the privilege of meeting and writing about influential pioneers from Roc-A-Fella's co-founder Damon Dash to the ubiquitous Quincy Jones. And it all began with *The Radical View*.

About the Idea

Shoot 'em up, bang bang! Violence in American movies has always been a hot-button issue in the black community. As a writer, I wanted to tell a positive, uplifting story about urban life. I wanted to show conflict without showing more black-on-black crime. Here's why: In the early nineties, gangster rap was spreading like wildfire through our music, movies and our culture. As I watched images of thugs and roughneck characters fill the big and small screens, I asked myself, "What would happen if one of these tough guys had to survive outside of their environment? How would he respond if he were forced to leave 'the hood' in order to stand up for something he believed in?"

Additionally, I noticed a pattern in urban films coming out of Hollywood. It seemed to me that the only story Hollywood knew how to produce was the one about a young black man torn between a life of crime or a career in rap music. Give me a break. Even when we were slaves we had more choices in life. I knew there were many more complex stories to be told about urban life. Thankfully, we now have a rich mix of urban storytellers like Tyler Perry, George Tillman, Jr. and Kasi Lemmons.

My story idea began with my longing for the south and my not-yet-acquired appreciation for the beaches of South Bay. My passion was so strong, I finished the first draft in seven days. I'd love to tell you that on the eighth day I rested, but no such luck. You see, I didn't own a TV and I couldn't afford to go to the movies. I had nothing else to do but start on the rewrite. Here's a tip for fellow scribes: If you want to avoid writer's block, ditch your TV. Whenever I got stuck on a scene or story point, I had to dig my way out. I couldn't pretend I would find the answers watching music videos or sitcom reruns. Then, I stayed at my desk and solved my story issues. Now, not so much. Especially now that I own a 42" flat screen high-definition TV.

About the Story

The Radical View is a drama about Brandon Bell, an angry, young black man with a prison record and a quest to find out why his successful brother Vernon committed suicide. Determined to bury his brother close to home, Brandon travels from the low-income section of Atlanta, formerly known as Bankhead Highway, to Palos Verdes, a posh community in California's South Bay area. Brandon is certain that his white sister-in-law Ashley is the reason Vernon killed himself.

"Can't we all just get along?" When Rodney King uttered those words to calm LA rioters, *The Radical View* was making its way through Hollywood. I am certain that executives liked the script because of its positive, non-violent perspective on race relations, which was particularly important while the riot wounds were still fresh.

In addition to the story arriving at the right time, it was equipped with two universal elements: 1) A streetwise and book smart main character with the ability to mingle with the boys in the hood and match wits with the educated elite. 2) An unsolved mystery driven by Brandon's burning desire to know why his big brother and idol gave up on life. Especially since Vernon was a successful attorney. Plus, Brandon wants to fulfill his mother's request to bring his brother's body home to Atlanta but he's not sure how he can logistically make it happen. Brandon's plight transcends race.

But when it comes to race, *The Radical View* touches on the problem of blacks assimilating into a predominantly white world without losing their heritage, friends and family. What's more, the story deals with an interracial relationship as told through Ashley's point of view. Brandon initially believes that Ashley and Vernon's relationship is superficial. As the story unfolds, his view changes.

Lastly, let mirth and laughter come. The script is filled with funny moments. I discovered early on in my writing career that the best dramas have their fair share of humor. Actually, I learned that technique from studying Shakespeare's tragedies in college.

About You

If you're reading this because you're an aspiring writer, here's my advice: Start your career by writing something that will move people. Too often young writers are told to write something that will sell. I say write stories that are emotionally close to your heart and the money will follow. If you're reading this because you enjoy reading great stories, bless you. I wish I could clone you. I hope that you'll discover nuances in the story and the characters that will touch you in the same way *The Radical View* has touched so many others over the past two decades.

Gregory LeGrand Kerns
May, 2008
Jersey City, New Jersey

Original cast from the staged reading of
THE RADICAL VIEW
December 10, 1991
Universal Studios, Hollywood, CA

Music by MICHAEL MIKLOS Produced by GEOFFREY H. MILLER
Written and Directed by GREGORY LEGRAND KERNS

Brandon Bell........................MICHAEL ANTHONY RAWLINS
Clarice Bell.......................................BRENDA LEAVITT
Henry Bell.......................................ORLANDO BONNER
Curb...DAVID P. LEWIS
Stan ....PAUL DAVID BRYANT
Hamp...BALDWIN SYKES
Derrius..HAVEN MITCHELL
Peanut...CHARLES ALLEN
Panther Lewis...............................MICHAEL VENSON
Frank McCormick ....ARLAND RUSSELL
Victoria.......................................LYNN A. HENDERSON
Ashley Bell...ANN NYBERG
John...WES COLE
Ice Cream Clerk...........................BRONWYN ST. JOHN
Mitch..STEVEN BASIL
Mailman.......................................HAVEN MITCHELL
Thomas..BALDWIN SYKES
Mary...REGINA RYER
Surfer Guy....................................GARY WORDHAM
Attractive Female............................BRONWYN ST. JOHN
Middle-Aged Male............................GARY WORDHAM
Carol...MARGARET ROMERO
First Doctor..................................BRONWYN ST. JOHN
Second Doctor................................BALDWIN SYKES
Harold..ARLAND RUSSELL
Sherwood..GARY WORDHAM
Robber..DAVID P. LEWIS
Operator......................................BRONWYN ST. JOHN
Cabbie...PAUL DAVID BRYANT
Narrator...DANI BALLEW

THE RADICAL VIEW

by

Gregory LeGrand Kerns

FADE IN:

EXT. PALM TREE - MORNING

On the start of a hazy California January day, a gentle
breeze sweeps across the ocean, subtly blowing the palm tree.

INT. MERCEDES SEDAN IN A DIMLY LIT GARAGE

Low angle from the back of the car. We see a man's legs in a
nice suit and Alligator shoes, step out of the house, open
the car door, get in and slam the door closed.

All is quiet and still as the CAMERA rises slowly to reveal
the back of the man's silhouetted head. Inside the car he
raises his left hand, points a gun to his temple and fires.

                                              CUT BACK TO:

EXT. PALM TREE - SAME

Blowing wildly as the GUNSHOT rings out over the ocean.

EXT. SCENES AROUND BANKHEAD (IN ATLANTA) - AFTERNOON

EXT. CONVENIENCE STORE FRONT - SAME

THREE LITTLE BOYS, all just under ten and black, bolt out of
the store and take off down the street.

The STORE CLERK runs out with a baseball bat, feverishly
shouts at the kids (MOS) while waving the bat in the air. A
dramatic R&B song with lyrics about ghetto life enhances the
visuals.

EXT. SIDEWALK IN FRONT OF A SCHOOL - DAY

In the same part of town. A group of BLACK MALE TEENAGERS
with school books are crowded around two boys as they face
off for a fight. The crowd encourages them to fight, but
nothing is happening.

Someone pushes one of the fighters into the other and the
fight is ignited. The two boys punch and slug one another
like barbarians. They wrestle each other to the ground and
the surrounding kids enjoy cheering them on.

EXT. SECLUDED GHETTO STREET - SAME

TWO BLACK MALES in their twenties step out into the middle of
the street. A van marked ATLANTA PACKAGE EXPRESS comes down
the street and stops in front of the two men.

They pull out guns and make the driver get out. They point
the gun at the driver's head while he opens the back. The
ROBBERS get mad when they rip open the only three packages in
the van and discover papers, dishes and ladies' clothing.

EXT. TRASHED OUT ALLEY - SAME

A couple of old, homeless, black WINOS are going through the
trash cans looking for food. One finds a McDonald's bag with
a half-eaten hamburger in it but refuses to share it with the
other. They are almost comical as they wrestle with the
piece of hamburger, each trying to get it in their own mouth.

From around the corner, come the THREE LITTLE BOYS on the run
from their convenience store heist. They frighten the Winos
into dropping the food, chase them away and claim the alley.
One of the kids steps on and smashes the hamburger. The boys
pull candy out of their underwear and socks and eat it. As
the music continues...

EXT. PACKAGE EXPRESS LOADING DOCK - DAY

All of the EMPLOYEES are engaged in an intense game of Nerf
basketball except for one. He is hiding behind a copy of the
underground newspaper, THE RADICAL VIEW.

BRANDON BELL lowers the paper, walks to the edge of the dock
and looks out down the street. He is a handsome twenty-six-
year-old black male.

As he searches the street for incoming deliveries we see that
he is definitely a young man with a lot on his mind.

From down the street comes the Package Express Van and it
pulls up to the dock. The Driver is visibly spooked from the
hold up. Brandon opens the back of the van and sees the
opened packages and destroyed goods. He slams his hand on
the van and curses to himself.

INT. TIME CLOCK - LATER

Brandon clocks out, puts his head phones on and dashes out of
the building like a fugitive on a jail break.

Once away from the work place, he loosens up as he bops to the rap MUSIC piercing his ears from the Walkman. Brandon heads toward the train station.

INT. TRAIN STATION - MOMENTS LATER

Brandon watches the people, mostly black males, coming and going as he waits for the train.

EXT. BANKHEAD COURT PROJECTS - LATER

Brandon enters the foreground of the screen, walks up to the front door of his home and enters.

INT. LIVING ROOM - SAME

HENRY BELL, a large man in his late fifties, stands in front of the TV, fiddling with the DVD player while holding a beer.

The living room is decorated with inexpensive traditional ethnic American art and furniture. The song fades down but not out. Brandon enters and walks right by his father. Henry looks up at his son.

                         HENRY
             You don't know how to speak?

Brandon disappears into his room. CLARICE BELL, Brandon's small-framed but stern mother, calls from the kitchen.

                         CLARICE (O.S.)
             Henry, was that Brandon?

                         HENRY
                (irritated)
             I told y'all not to put this piece
             of junk in here! I can't even
             watch simple TV. I know why he
             sent it, but it ain't gonna work.
             He trying to make up for that girl.

Clarice comes out of the kitchen.

                         CLARICE
             What's the matter, Honey?

                         HENRY
             He tryin' to say it's for our 30th
             wedding anniversary. I ain't
             stupid.
                         (more)

                    HENRY (cont'd)
          I ain't go to no fancy school like
          USCLA or wherever it was he went,
          but I ain't stupid.

Clarice comes over, presses two buttons and gets the TV to
work and exits. Henry stands dumbfounded.

INT. BRANDON'S ROOM - SAME

He takes off his work uniform and changes into his street
clothes. A hooded sweatshirt, a leather jacket and a
baseball cap. He puts a notepad in his pocket.

INT. LIVING ROOM - SAME

Brandon comes back through the living room. Clarice catches
him on his way out.

                    CLARICE
                 (with caution)
          Dinner is ready, if you're hungry.

Brandon turns and goes into the kitchen and grabs a piece of
chicken off the stove and puts it in his mouth. He grabs a
biscuit and a can of soda out of the refrigerator and heads
for the door.

Henry sees Brandon walking through the living room with the
food in his mouth and sits up in his chair.

                    HENRY
          Damn, boy! Sit yo butt down and
          fix you a plate like you got some
          sense!

Brandon is out the door.

EXT. CITY STREETS - EARLY EVENING

The song comes back in strong as Brandon walks down the
street finishing his chicken. He takes the bone and throws
it over his shoulder.

EXT. RUNDOWN APARTMENT BUILDING - MOMENTS LATER

Brandon walks up to an apartment door and KNOCKS. A GIRL
opens the door and lets him in.

INT. BEDROOM - LATER IN THE NIGHT

Brandon, in the girl's bed, stares at the ceiling. The
CAMERA moves in slowly before we...

                                                   CUT TO:

VISUAL FLASHBACK MONTAGE (SLOW MOTION)

of Brandon in his prison cell.

Brandon has a haunting nightmare of being held at gunpoint by
several FACELESS GUNMEN.

Violence in the neighborhood. DOMESTIC FIGHTS, DRIVE-BY
SHOOTINGS, and Brandon in a serious KNIFE FIGHT.

                                                   BACK TO:

THE BEDROOM - SAME NIGHT

The Girl cuddles up to Brandon and he snaps out of the
trance. He looks over and the clock says 3:00 a.m. He gets
up and she tries to pull him back in bed.

EXT. APARTMENT BUILDING - SAME NIGHT

Brandon comes out, still putting on his clothes and headed
down the street.

EXT. CITY ROOF TOP - EARLY MORNING

Brandon sits with a pen and notepad watching the sunrise.

EXT. STREET CORNER HANG OUT - DAY

HAMP, DERRIUS, and PEANUT sit with Brandon, wasting time.
Brandon writes in his notepad. A Police car drives by
slowly. The two black males who held up the Package Express
van, CURB and STAN, approach them.

                         CURB
               Yo, Stan, my man, look who it is,
               back on the block!

                    STAN
          Brandon Bell and his stinkin' ass!!
          Curb, what's up with that?

Peanut, a short black male, dressed in a sweat suit and gold
chains, has a missing front tooth and a gold cap on another
one, jumps up in Brandon's defense.

                    PEANUT
          Curb, man, you and Stan need to go
          on somewhere. We don't wanna have
          nuttin' to do with y'all.

                    CURB
               (pushes him back down)
          Sit your little black ass down,
          Peanut.

Brandon looks up.

                    STAN
          Yeah, we'll call you when we ready
          for a peanut butter and jelly
          sandwich.

They move in close to Brandon.

                    CURB
          Yo, 'B'... so what's up?

Curb studies Brandon closely.

                    BRANDON
          Nothing.

                    STAN
          We want you to help us with
          something.

They examine him closer for a response. Stan gives him a
light chuck on the shoulder.

                    STAN (cont'd)
          Five years, your arm oughta be as
          good as new.

                    CURB
          There's a little danger involved.
          You with it?

Brandon shakes his head 'no'.

                    STAN
          Afraid?

                    CURB
          They tell me once you kill a man
          you ain't afraid of nothing.

Brandon stares him down. Peanut jumps up again.

                    PEANUT
          And he ain't afraid to kill you
          mother fuckers!!

                    BRANDON
          Yo, Peanut.

He shakes his head for Peanut to chill out. Peanut sits
down.   Curb and Stan back off.

                    STAN
          He ain't down. He done gone soft.
          I can see it all over his face.

                    CURB
          Yeah, he might as well move to
          California with his punk ass
          brother.

                    STAN
          Later for you pussies. Yo, Curb,
          let's exit.

They take off. Brandon jumps up and paces the turf, as he
tries extremely hard not to explode.

                    BRANDON
          Mother fuckers just like that are
          gonna make me end up back in
          prison.

INT. LIVING ROOM - NIGHT

Henry watches TV with a drink in his hand. Brandon enters
and goes in the kitchen. He comes out with a big bag of
cookies, a gallon of milk and a large plastic cup.

                    HENRY
          Brandon.

Brandon stops. Henry gets up and walks over to him.

>   HENRY (cont'd)
>   Where were you last night? You
>   been out stealing with that boy
>   Curb?

Trying to withstand the ridicule, Brandon looks away, takes a deep breath and releases a heavy sigh. Henry gets furious and pushes him hard across his right shoulder. Brandon bites his lip in excruciating pain.

>   HENRY (cont'd)
>   Listen, boy! Your parole officer
>   made me responsible for you! And I
>   ain't gonna have you out there
>   running around with those hoodlums.

>   BRANDON
>   (still in pain)
>   I wasn't!!

Henry snatches him by the collar.

>   HENRY
>   Then why the hell didn't you answer
>   me?!

He slams Brandon up against the wall. The milk and cookies go everywhere. Brandon struggles to break free.

>   BRANDON
>   Let go!!

Henry throws him in an arm lock and pins his face against the wall.

>   BRANDON (cont'd)
>   (near tears)
>   Dad... my arm!

>   HENRY
>   No, you wanna stay out in the
>   streets all night but I ain't gonna
>   have it! Hear me, boy?!

Henry puts a tighter grip on Brandon's arm.

>   HENRY (cont'd)
>   You wanna go back to prison?!

>   BRANDON
>   NO!!!!

Clarice enters.

                    CLARICE
          Henry!!

                    HENRY
          Vernon never got into trouble!!

She pulls Henry off of him. Brandon falls to the floor and
stretches his arm to ease the pain.

                    HENRY (cont'd)
          In my house, you play by my rules,
          God Damn it!!

Clarice tries to restrain Henry. Brandon gets up and dashes
out the front door.

                    HENRY (cont'd)
          That boy has got to learn to
          listen!!

                    CLARICE
          And you've got to stop beatin' on
          him!

EXT. STREET CORNER HANG OUT - NEXT DAY

Peanut, Hamp and Derrius relax at their usual hangout.
Brandon paces the turf.

                    BRANDON
          The next time he puts his hands on
          me... I swear...

                    HAMP
          I know, man, I gotta put up with
          the same shit from my old man.
          That's why I got this.

Hamp reveals a gun. Everyone is silenced by the thought of
Hamp defending himself from his father.

                    HAMP (cont'd)
          But I want you to take it.

Hamp extends it to Brandon.

                    BRANDON
          You crazy, man? I can't take that.

                    HAMP
          No, see, I got a cat coming 'round
          on Monday to give me a few dollars
          for it. I know if my old man gets
          drunk like he does every weekend
          and if this is around...

Brandon is well aware of what might happen. He takes the gun
from Hamp.

                    BRANDON
               (releases a frustrated
                sigh)
          Damn, I gotta get out of here!

                    DERRIUS
          You can't, man. It's like we still
          in prison.

                    BRANDON
          That's bullshit, Derrius. I'm
          gonna find me a way out.

                    DERRIUS
          Yeah, in a body bag.

                    BRANDON
          I ain't going out like that. I'm
          gonna be famous. Somebody great.

                    DERRIUS
          At what?

                    BRANDON
          Shit, I don't know. Something.

                    PEANUT
          I'm gonna be famous.
               (beat)
          Pimpin' Hos, slammin' Cadillac dos
          and puttin' anybody talkin' junk in
          the trunk.

He laughs at his own poetry.

                    BRANDON
          Maybe I could be like Victoria. Be
          a doctor and bring my shit back to
          the hood. I don't know.
               (beat)
          I even thought about being a
          rapper.

They all laugh at Brandon.

                      BRANDON (cont'd)
        Why not? I can be on stage. I can
        do that shit. Check it out.

Brandon jumps up and starts to dance. The fellas trip out
and make fun of the way he dances.

                      BRANDON (cont'd)
               (clowning around)
        Am I on it? Y'all can be my posse.
        One-two, One-two. Ah yeah, ah
        yeah!!

                      DERRIUS
        Not with you dancin' like that.

                      HAMP
        Man, you oughta go live with your
        brother Vernon.

                      DERRIUS
        Yeah, man. If I had the chance to
        go to Cali... shoot!! I'd go and
        never come back. What's up with
        that?

Brandon dances on.

                      DERRIUS (cont'd)
        You cats don't get along no more?

Brandon continues dancing to avoid the question.

                      HAMP
        Remember we use to see them running
        around here together like Willie
        Tyler and Lester? Everywhere
        Vernon went, Brandon was on his
        tip.

                      DERRIUS
        Now it's Peanut following you
        around everywhere.

                      PEANUT
        No I don't.

                      DERRIUS
        Shut up!
              (to Brandon)
        What happened?
                (more)

                    DERRIUS (cont'd)
          Vernon told you he didn't want no
          ex-cons in his house? That's it,
          ain't it?

Brandon stops.

                    BRANDON
          Hell no. He begged me to come out
          but I told him not while he was
          laying up with that snow girl.

                    DERRIUS
          So what you gonna do?

                    BRANDON
          I don't know.

                    PEANUT
          Man, you gonna be a writer, man.

                    BRANDON
               (not totally convinced)
          Yeah. All right, fellas, I've
          gotta bounce off to work.

They all tease him because he has to go to work.

                    BRANDON (cont'd)
          All right. I'll remember that shit
          on pay day when you mother fuckers
          are all up in my face wanting to
          hold some money.

Hamp comes up to Brandon.

                    HAMP
          Hey, Brandon. Thanks, man.

                    BRANDON
          No puzzle, my brother. No puzzle.

INT. LIVING ROOM - EVENING

Henry tries to watch TV over the loud rap MUSIC coming from
Brandon's room. The bass is so heavy the pictures on the wall
are vibrating.

                    HENRY
          Clarice! You better go in there...

Clarice enters from the kitchen, through the living room, up
to Brandon's door and knocks. She tries to open the locked
door.

                         CLARICE
              Brandon, Sweetheart, turn the music
              down.

INT. BEDROOM - SAME

Brandon is stretched out on the bed with the gun in his hand
and stares at the wall. Clarice continues to talk to him
from behind the door.

                         CLARICE (O.S.)
              That Panther guy called. And
              Vernon called. He wants you to
              call him back.
                   (she waits for a response)
              Also your parole officer called to
              see how you were doing.

                         BRANDON
                   (to himself)
              Lousy, what does he expect. How in
              the hell is a man supposed to
              reform and rehabilitate when he has
              to come back to the same
              environment that got him in
              trouble.

                                        CUT BACK TO:

LIVING ROOM

Clarice moves away from the door.

                         HENRY
              That boy is trying my patience.

She joins Henry in the living room and perches with tension
on the corner of the couch.

                         CLARICE
              Henry, when Vernon called, he said
              he and Ashley were coming to
              Atlanta next month. He wants us to
              meet her.

                         HENRY
              He better check into a hotel.

                         CLARICE
                   (ashamed of him)
              A hotel?

14.

                    HENRY
          He can afford it. He knows how I
          feel about crackers.

Clarice is hurt by her husband's words but is unsure how to
approach the subject.

                    CLARICE
          But we ain't even met her yet.

                    HENRY
          Do we have to talk about this now?
          I'm trying to watch TV.
               (screams over his
                shoulder)
          BRANDON, TURN THAT JUNGLE MUSIC
          DOWN!!!

Clarice throws up her hands and exits.

INT. BRANDON'S BEDROOM - SAME

Brandon examines the gun. He aims it at several things
around the room and pretends to shoot them. He puts the gun
to his temple, closes his eyes and pretends to pull the
trigger. He opens his eyes and sees himself in the mirror on
the dresser.

                    BRANDON
               (to the mirror)
          What are you looking at?

He points the gun at the mirror.

                                        CUT BACK TO:

INT. LIVING ROOM - SAME

A GUNSHOT is heard, glass breaks and a bullet comes through
the wall and knocks a picture off the wall.

Clarice screams and Henry jumps up, runs and kicks Brandon's
door in and sees the shattered mirror on the floor.

Brandon is shaken by the fact that the gun went off.
Clarice, in the background, screams, and cries praises to the
Lord.

                    HENRY
          WHAT THE HELL IS GOING ON IN
          HERE?!!

                        BRANDON
          It went off.

                        HENRY
                 (so mad he can barely spit
                  his words out)
          WHAT IN THE HELL ARE YOU DOING WITH
          A GUN?!! You ain't suppose to have
          no weapons! You wanna end up dead
          or back in prison, that's what you
          want, ain't it?!!

Clarice is in the background, hysterical.

                        HENRY (cont'd)
          I swear, I'm gone send you to live
          with Vernon! Maybe he can knock
          some sense into yo' hard-ass-head!!

Henry continues to rant and rave in the doorway while Clarice
still wails in the living room. The phone beside Brandon's
bed RINGS.

                        HENRY (cont'd)
          If that's one of your girlfriends
          you just better tell her to forget
          about it tonight.

                        BRANDON
          Hello.

                        FRANK (O.S.)
          May I speak with Mr. Bell, please.

Brandon looks at his father who is now in the living room
comforting Clarice. He rolls over and turns his back to
them.

                        BRANDON
          Speaking.

                        FRANK
          Mr. Bell, this is Frank McCormick
          from the McCormick Brothers
          Mortuary in Los Angeles. We regret
          to inform you that your son Vernon
          is deceased.

                        BRANDON
                 (sits up)
          What?!

                         FRANK
               Cause of death was an apparent
               suicide.

Brandon stands up and drops the phone on the bed. He
staggers from the emotional shock, out of the bedroom and
into the living room where Henry tries to get Clarice to calm
down.

The CAMERA remains in the bedroom as Brandon tells his
parents the news (MOS). Henry picks up the phone. Brandon,
physically weak from the news, returns to the bedroom and
wanders emotionally confused before exploding all of his
anger onto a defenseless dresser lamp. Unable to stand up
any longer, he collapses on the bed.

EXT. TWO-STORY, OLD OFFICE BUILDING - DAY

Peanut tags along behind Brandon as they enter the building.

INT. SMALL, VERY CLUTTERED OFFICE - DAY

Behind the junk-filled desk is PANTHER LEWIS, a large,
physically intimidating black man with a kind face. He works
on a computer, the only state-of-the-art equipment in the
office of the underground newspaper, *The Radical View*.

Brandon and Peanut enter. Panther stops his work to greet
them.

                         PANTHER
               Hey, man, I'm sorry about your
               brother.

They shake hands and hug.

                         PEANUT
               Ain't dat some shit?

                         BRANDON
               Yo, Panther, this is my homey,
               Peanut. Peanut, Panther Lewis. I
               met Panther in the joint.

                         PANTHER
               You cats just in time to give me a
               hand.

Panther hands them each a large bundle of newspapers.

                    PEANUT
          Yo, Panther, man, that's some
          serious shit you be running down in
          your paper. Like about the March
          on Washington. How the man
          couldn't stop the grass roots
          niggers from stampeding the Capitol
          so they took over the show. I
          learn all kinds of shit from your
          paper.

                    PANTHER
          I appreciate you reading it.

                    PEANUT
          Oh, I don't be readin' it. Brandon
          be schoolin' me.

                    PANTHER
          Why don't you read it for yourself?

                    PEANUT
          'Cause I cain't.

                    PANTHER
          An illiterate black man. That
          breaks my heart. I don't wanna
          lecture you, my young brother, but
          you gotta learn to read.

                    BRANDON
             (ashamed for him)
          I'm teaching him.

They make their way out of the office and Panther locks the
door as they continue down the hall.

                    PEANUT
          Maybe it don't pay to learn to
          read. Shit, Vernon went to law
          school, had a big money gig, a nice
          crib, nice wheels and he still
          killed himself. What's up with
          that? All of a sudden my life is
          lookin' damn good. Ill-literature
          and all.

                    BRANDON
          Illiterate.

                    PEANUT
          Shit, that, too.

EXT. OFFICE BUILDING - DAY

The three men come out of the building and proceed down the
street. Panther occasionally hands papers to people on the
street.

                    PANTHER
               (to Brandon)
          Let me know if I can do anything.

                    BRANDON
          My folks wanna bury him here so I'm
          trying to scrape up a few dollars
          to bring his body back.

They stop at the corner before crossing the street.

                    PEANUT
          I gave 'em three dollars. I would
          given him more but my baby mama's
          check ain't come in yet.

Panther gives Peanut a look that says 'what's he gonna do
with fifty cents?' Throws his arms up in the air.

                    PEANUT (cont'd)
          Dat's all I had, my brother.

They cross the street.

                    PANTHER
          Yeah, man, I can't pay you but I
          can swing a few dollars for a
          cause.

                    BRANDON
          That'll work.

The threesome enter a...

INT. SMALL ETHNIC BOOK STORE - CONTINUOUS

They drop off the newspapers.

                    PANTHER
          Now what's up with these stories
          I've been hearing about you and
          that doctor we did a piece on?

                    PEANUT
          Victoria?! That Ho is bad! 'B'
          all over that shit, too, man!

                    PANTHER
          Oh, he is?

                    BRANDON
          She's just a friend.

                    PEANUT
              (to Panther)
          Hey, man, you know the bitch is bad
          if he's known her for three weeks
          and he ain't smoked them panties
          yet. But he still after her.

                    PANTHER
          Yeah?

                    PEANUT
          And you know how it is when you get
          out of the joint. Your dick be so
          hard it takes two years and two
          hundred Hos to make it go down. So
          'B', what's up with that?

                    BRANDON
          She ain't a bitch, and she ain't a
          ho. She's a lady.

                    PEANUT
          Ladies need their panties smoked,
          too.

INT. PANTHER'S OFFICE - MOMENTS LATER

Panther opens a strong box, pulls out a hundred dollar bill
and gives it to Brandon.

                    PANTHER
          Listen, man, you got anything I can
          print before you sky up?

Brandon reaches in his pocket and retrieves some folded
notepad sheets.

                    BRANDON
          Yeah. I wrote this piece about us.
          About how we educated ourselves in
          the pen.

                    PANTHER
          Solid.
               (looks at the wadded
               paper)
          Man, you gotta at least get you a
          typewriter.

                    PEANUT
          I told him I'd steal one for him.

                    BRANDON
          My next piece is gonna be about why
          brothers have such low self-esteem.

                    PEANUT
          Low self-esteem? What's dat?

                    PANTHER
          That's when you don't think much of
          yourself.

                    PEANUT
          I can write a story on that. It's
          because a brother ain't got shit to
          look forward to.

                    PANTHER
          What about Vernon? He had a lot to
          look forward to. Why did he commit
          suicide?

Brandon ponders the question.

                    PANTHER (cont'd)
          Maybe that's what your next piece
          should be about.

EXT. TRAIN STATION - MOMENTS LATER

Brandon and Peanut enter the station and head toward the
platform.

                    PEANUT
          Damn, man, I wish I were in your
          shoes.

                    BRANDON
          Why?

                    PEANUT
          You 'bout to get a whole lot of
          free shit.

Brandon stops.

                    BRANDON
          What?

                    PEANUT
          First thing you do is go through
          his closets and get all his
          clothes. Get the keys to his Benzo
          and see if he left any money laying
          around. Then get his American
          Express card and charge up a bunch
          of shit before they find out he's
          gone. I'm serious, man. You 'bout
          to get paid.

                    BRANDON
          You want me to wear my dead
          brother's clothes?

                    PEANUT
          Shit yeah! If it ain't got no
          bullet holes in it. I've gotten
          some of my best suits from dead
          men.

A Southbound train comes on the other side of the platform
and Brandon turns toward the train.

                    BRANDON
          You a sick mother fucker. Look,
          I'll catch you later.

                    PEANUT
          Why you catching that train? Where
          you going?

                    BRANDON
          None of your business.

                    PEANUT
          I know where you going. I can see
          it in yo' eyes.

                    BRANDON
          You don't see a damn thing in my
          eyes but my eyeballs.

Brandon jumps on board, the doors close and the train pulls
out.

INT. CLINIC - DAY

The place is small, clean and neatly decorated. Brandon
enters and makes his way back to one of the offices. He pops
his head in the doorway. VICTORIA, an attractive, confident,
well-dressed black woman in her late twenties, looks up from
her desk and smiles when she sees him.

                    BRANDON
          What's up, Doc?

                    VICTORIA
          How's it going?

Brandon enters and immediately begins pacing the room.

                    BRANDON
          My arm's been hurtin' a bit but I'm
          okay.

Victoria moves toward him.

                    VICTORIA
          Let me look at it.

Brandon takes his jacket and shirt off as she examines him.

                    VICTORIA (cont'd)
          You holding up okay?

                    BRANDON
          I'm going to California and I need
          a favor.

Victoria studies his face.

                    VICTORIA
          You're going for the wrong reason.
          I can tell.

                    BRANDON
          Victoria, don't try and lay any
          free clinic reasoning on me.
          Vernon was fine the last time I
          talked to him.

                    VICTORIA
          And when was that?

Victoria waits for his answer because they know it's been a
long time.

                    BRANDON
               (losing his cool)
          It's my brother that's out there!!
               (returning to earth)
          Look, I just need you to take me to
          the airport. Can you do that or is
          it going to cost me a lecture?

                    VICTORIA
          I just don't want you to set
          yourself back another five years.

                    BRANDON
          So you just want me to let those
          white people do whatever they want
          to with my brother's body?

Victoria ends the examination and returns to her desk.

                    VICTORIA
          Fine, let that chip on your
          shoulder get you into trouble. I
          don't care. It's been nice knowing
          you because I'll probably never see
          you again.

                    BRANDON
          Probably not. I may get shot in
          Cali by some dope fiend.

Brandon sees that Victoria is uncomfortable with his words.

                    BRANDON (cont'd)
          I'm coming back.
               (beat)
          My parole officer says I have to.

                    VICTORIA
          That's the only reason?

                    BRANDON
               (thinks a moment)
          Well, no, I'm coming back for my
          check-ups.

Victoria realizes that he's playing hard to get.

                    VICTORIA
          Oh, okay then.

                    BRANDON
          And I'm coming back to see Peanut.

                    VICTORIA
          Then you let Peanut take you to the
          airport.

                    BRANDON
          I can't because Peanut don't know
          how to drive.

                    VICTORIA
          Get out of here. I have work to
          do.

Brandon starts to exit but stops at the door and looks back.

                    BRANDON
          Victoria, I'm coming back to see
          you.

Victoria smiles and Brandon flashes her a smile in return and
exits.

INT. BELL LIVING ROOM - NIGHT

Brandon is seated on the couch with his foot propped up on
the coffee table, on the telephone. He scribbles some
figures in his notepad.

                    BRANDON
                 (on the phone)
          That's the cheapest...?

He hangs up the phone.

                    BRANDON (cont'd)
          Damn, for that I can buy a car,
          drive out there and have change
          left over.

Henry enters.

                    HENRY
          Boy, take your foot off the
          furniture.

Brandon removes his foot. Henry sits down and pulls some
cash out of his pocket.

                    HENRY (cont'd)
          This is all we could come up with.
          It'll get you out there. Next week
          when I get paid, I'll try and wire
          you something to get home with.

                          BRANDON
            It's cheaper if I buy a round-trip
            ticket.

                          HENRY
            But we ain't got no round-trip
            money.

Henry gives him the money.

                          HENRY (cont'd)
            She know you coming?

                          BRANDON
            Not yet.

Brandon takes a deep breath, looks up the number in the
address book by the phone and reaches for the phone but
before he can pick it up it RINGS. He answers it.

                          BRANDON (cont'd)
            Hello.

INT. ASHLEY'S HOUSE - DAY

Ashley's on the phone, on the couch.

INTERCUT:

                          ASHLEY
            Hello, is this Brandon?

                          BRANDON
            Yeah, what's up?

                          ASHLEY
            This is Ashley.
                (proceeds with caution)
            I'm sorry about everything. I was
            up visiting my parents in Santa
            Barbara. I came home and found
            him. I would have called earlier
            but it's been crazy here.

                          BRANDON
            I was just about to call and let
            you know I was coming out.

                          ASHLEY
                (with frailness in
                her voice)
                    (more)

                    ASHLEY (cont'd)
          That's really nice. Are your
          parents coming, too?

                    BRANDON
          No, just me.

                    ASHLEY
          They should try and make it out.
          The funeral's not until Saturday.

                    BRANDON
          The funeral?

                    HENRY
          The funeral? Clarice, you better
          get in here.

                    BRANDON
          We're having his funeral here.

                    ASHLEY
               (after a moment of
               silent surprise)
          But everything's being taken care
          of out here. Don't worry, my
          father's covering all the expenses.

     Clarice enters and stands over Henry.

                    BRANDON
               (with an attitude)
          Yeah, but his family wants him
          buried here.

                    ASHLEY
          He has family here now. I am his
          wife.

                    CLARICE
          She's not gonna let me bring my
          baby home?

                    BRANDON
               (sensing his mother's
               anxiety)
          Look, he's my brother and my
          parents want him buried here. If
          your old man wants to shell out
          some dough, then he can pay for my
          plane ticket out there.

                        ASHLEY
              (hurt fills her voice
              with tears, she tries to
              hold back)
          We haven't even heard from you guys
          in two years. You wouldn't even
          return his phone calls!

                        BRANDON
          Fuck that!! I'm coming out there
          to get his body and I don't give a
          damn what you and your family
          think.

Brandon slams the phone down. Boiling with anger, he jumps
up and bounces around the room.

                        BRANDON (cont'd)
          Who does that bitch think she is?!

                        CLARICE
              (accepting the blame)
          I knew we were being too hard on
          him.

                        HENRY
              (tries to convince
              Clarice)
          It ain't our fault.

                        CLARICE
          We could have let him stay here.

                        HENRY
          We ain't taking the blame for this!
          Hell no!!

                        CLARICE
              (near tears)
          Brandon, Honey?

                        BRANDON
          Yes, Mama.

                        CLARICE
          Come here.

He moves to her and she grabs him.

                        CLARICE (cont'd)
              (softly)
          Go out there and bring my baby back
          home, okay?

                         BRANDON
              Don't worry, Mama, I will. I will.

EXT. AIRPORT DROP-OFF SECTION - DAY

A late model luxury car pulls up and parks. Victoria gets
out of the driver's side. Brandon gets out of the
passenger's side. She opens the trunk and he grabs his
duffle bag.

                         BRANDON
                    (very cold)
              Thanks, Doc.

He starts to walk off. Victoria wants a better good-bye than
this.

                         VICTORIA
              Is that it?

                         BRANDON
              What?

                         VICTORIA
                    (resigned)
              Just be careful out there.

                         BRANDON
              I will.
                    (pause)
              All right, I'm out.

Brandon doesn't move. He wants to make a move but isn't sure
how to go about it. He musters his courage, drops his bag
and leans in and kisses Victoria for the first time.

                         BRANDON (cont'd)
              Good-bye.

                         VICTORIA
                    (teasing him)
              You knew that was what you were
              supposed to say all along.

He turns and walks toward the terminal. Victoria smiles as
she watches him exit.

EXT. DC-10 RISING INTO THE SKY - DAY

EXT. SERIES OF CALIFORNIA IMAGES - DAY

Ocean waves. The beach. Palm trees. The hillside mansions.
People eating ice cream. Birds flying above the line where
the ocean meets the sky.

Volleyball players and sun tanners line the beach while other
Californians rollerblade, bicycle, and jog along the coast.

EXT. SOUTH BAY YELLOW CAB - DAY

Winding up the Palos Verdes hills.

EXT. FRONT OF A HOUSE - LATER

The DRIVER parks, looks back at Brandon with suspicion.
Brandon pays the fare, grabs his bag and gets out. The
Driver watches him walk away. Brandon stops and gives the
Driver a 'you got a problem?' look. He drives off.

Brandon walks up the driveway and sees a basketball hoop
hangs above the garage. He looks in the garage window and
sees a Benz. He goes to the front door and rings the bell.
No answer. He sets down his bag, pulls out a wire
configuration, looks around and in a matter of seconds, pops
the lock open and enters.

INT. LIVING ROOM - SAME

The house is decorated with black leather, lacquer and glass
furniture accented by white accessories. Brandon looks
around and nods in approval of the decor. He moves over to
the mantle and looks at the pictures. Brandon smiles when he
sees a picture of him and Vernon together.

                                                    CUT TO:

EXT. SMALL SOUTH BAY ICE CREAM PARLOR - DAY

A late model foreign luxury car pulls up and parks. Out of
the passenger side steps ASHLEY BELL, an attractive white
female, wearing sunglasses and carrying a big plastic bottle
of water.

Ashley is small framed but not frail or petite. The way she
carries herself automatically reveals that she is visibly
stressed.

She closes the door and then checks to make sure it's locked
and it comes open. She reaches in to try and lock it again
and still no success. She stops, takes a deep, frustrated
breath. Before she can attempt the sequence again, MITCH, a
handsome, dapper man in his late thirties with a face
slightly tensed from concern for his sister, comes from the
other side of the car and locks the door with the remote.

INSIDE THE PARLOR - SAME

Ashley and Mitch approach the counter. THE CLERK comes from
the back room.

                    CLERK
          May I help you?

Ashley, still in her shades, looks up at all the choices of
flavors. Silence. The Clerk looks at her. Mitch looks at
her.

                    MITCH
               (kindly)
          Ashley, what do you want?

She releases a heavy 'I'm so confused about life' sigh.

                    ASHLEY
          I don't know.

                    MITCH
               (with confidence to
               the Clerk)
          Make it Rocky Road.

Ashley gives Mitch a look that says 'definitely not Rocky
Road'.

                    MITCH (cont'd)
          How about Cookies and Cream?

                    ASHLEY
          That'll work.

The Clerk scoops the ice cream and gives it to her. She goes
and sits at a table.

                    MITCH
          Make mine pistachio in a cup.
               (joking)
          Extra pistachios.

INT. HOUSE - SAME

Brandon hears a car pull up in the driveway. He freezes but doesn't flinch.

Brandon peeks out of the window and sees TOM, a geeky, clean cut, glasses-wearing black male, in his late twenties but with a face that suggests he might be younger. Tom walks up to the front door and rings the bell. Brandon opens the door with confidence.

>   BRANDON
>   Yes.

Tom is surprised to see him and panics but tries hard not to show it. He thinks that Brandon is Vernon.

>   TOM
>   Uh... Hi, I'm Tom... I thought
>   you... I heard that you... somebody
>   said... well, I was checking to
>   see if Ashley was okay. But if
>   you're fine--I mean if she's here--
>   I mean if you're here, I'm sure
>   she's fine. Well, nice chatting
>   with you. Have a good day.

He speed walks off the porch, across the lawn, to his car and peels out of the driveway.

Brandon finds that whole scene rather odd.

>   CUT BACK TO:

INT. ICE CREAM PARLOR - SAME

Mitch and Ashley sit at a table. Ashley just holds her ice cream cone.

>   MITCH
>   Dad wants you to come back up to
>   the house.

>   ASHLEY
>   He just wants to pamper me.

>   MITCH
>   If we go next weekend we can
>   probably get a taste of the goodies
>   from his deep sea fishing trip.

Mitch still tries to sell Ashley on the idea.

                    MITCH (cont'd)
          It's been too long since the whole
          family has been together.

Ashley finally licks her ice cream and it falls off the cone.
She is upset but tries not to show it.

                    MITCH (cont'd)
          I'll get you another.

                    ASHLEY
          No, it's okay.

Mitch takes the cone from her, grabs a napkin, swoops the ice
cream off the floor and throws it away on his way up to the
counter.

Ashley takes her shades off, and presses her fingers to her
forehead to try and restrain an emotional outburst. Mitch
returns with ice cream and cone all in a cup.

                    ASHLEY (cont'd)
          I've been trying to put it all out
          of my mind and get on with my life
          but I just can't. There are so
          many unanswered questions.

She takes her plastic spoon and demolishes the cone in the
cup, subconsciously releasing her pain on the cone.

                    MITCH
          Maybe we should try and get you
          another journalist job abroad. You
          liked South Africa.

                    ASHLEY
          I can't leave the country right
          now.
            (beat)
          Besides, I've pretty much decided,
          to be a half-way decent journalist
          you have to enjoy writing.

She pushes her ice cream away and puts her shades back on.
Mitch reaches out and massages her shoulder.

                    ASHLEY (cont'd)
          I was doing okay until I talked to
          his brother.

INT. LIVING ROOM - DAY

Brandon sits on the couch, waiting patiently. He thinks for
a second and then gets up and goes out the front door, locks
it and waits on the front porch.

EXT. FRONT OF THE HOUSE - DAY

Mitch's car comes down the street and parks in front of the
house. He turns to Ashley.

                    MITCH
          Are you sure you're not afraid to
          be in the house alone?

                    ASHLEY
              (she is but doesn't
              want him to know)
          I'm sure. Carol might stop by
          later.

They kiss each other on the cheek.

                    ASHLEY (cont'd)
          Love you.

                    MITCH
          Love you, too.

Ashley grabs her bottle of water and gets out of the car.
She watches him drive off, turns and heads toward the porch.
She glances up and is startled when she sees Brandon on the
porch staring at her.

                    ASHLEY
          Who are you?

                    BRANDON
          You must be my mother fuckin'
          sister-in-law.

She already senses trouble as she walks by him to unlock the
door.

                    ASHLEY
          What do you want?

                    BRANDON
          That's a stupid ass question.

She unlocks the door and enters. He throws his duffle bag on his shoulder and falls in behind her.

INSIDE THE HOUSE

                    BRANDON
          What do you think I want?

                    ASHLEY
          Trouble.

                    BRANDON
               (slave dialect)
          'No Miss Ann, I's don't wants no
          trouble.' I just want to get my
          business taken care of and get the
          hell out of here. I would check
          into a hotel but I can't afford it,
          so I'm staying here.

                    ASHLEY
          What if I don't want you to stay
          here?

                    BRANDON
          You don't have a choice. This is
          my brother's house.

                    ASHLEY
               (correcting him)
          This was my husband's house, which
          means I own it now.

                    BRANDON
          I don't recall a will being read.
          You may be surprised, he probably
          didn't leave you a damn thing. So
          don't jump to any conclusions. Now
          I ain't gonna be here long so while
          I'm here, you don't say shit to me,
          and I won't say shit to you.
               (weary)
          I've never flown before and this
          jet lag is kicking my ass. I'm
          going to bed.

He picks up his bag and starts down the hall. She follows him.

                    ASHLEY
          I've got a few house rules.
          Everything you need is in the extra
          bathroom, so you don't need to go
          through my closets. If you have to
          use the kitchen, you better buy
          your own food. And I don't want
          you eating what I cook.

                    BRANDON
          My Doctor told me it was bad for my
          health to eat white food.

EXT. ASHLEY'S HOUSE - NIGHT

Establishing shot.

INT. DIMLY LIT KITCHEN - NIGHT

Ashley sits at the table eating a salad and reading
Cosmopolitan. Brandon enters in shorts, bare feet, a torn
tank top and carrying a cup.

On Brandon's upper right arm he has a very nasty scar from a
knife wound. He stops when he sees Ashley at the table.
They stare at each other.

                    BRANDON
          May I have some of your water? I
          brought my own cup.

                    ASHLEY
               What kind?

                    BRANDON
               A plastic cup.

                    ASHLEY
          No, what kind of water?

                    BRANDON
          Water you drink. It's free, ain't
          it?

                    ASHLEY
          Not in California. I've got
          sparkling, flat, flavored, bottled
          or tap. None of it's free.

                    BRANDON
          Which is cheapest?

                    ASHLEY
          Tap. But it's not cold like the
          bottled water. Do you want cold
          water?

                    BRANDON
          Yeah, but if it's going to cost me
          extra...

                    ASHLEY
          Have some of the bottled water in
          the fridge. No charge.

                    BRANDON
               (exasperated)
          Damn!

                    ASHLEY
          Is that how you guys say thank you
          in Atlanta?

He opens the refrigerator and sees a wide assortment of
waters.

                    BRANDON
          We don't make such a big deal over
          water.

Brandon stands in the middle of the kitchen and pours the
water into his cup and drinks it. Ashley can't help but
stare at his scar. He finishes his water and notices her.

                    BRANDON (cont'd)
          What the hell are you staring at?
          You never seen a thirsty man
          before?

                    ASHLEY
          It's amazing how much you resemble
          Vernon. I look at you and I see
          him.

                    BRANDON
          Well I ain't fuckin' Vernon.

                    ASHLEY
          And when you open your trash mouth,
          it brings me right back to reality.

Brandon exits. Ashley returns to her magazine.

INT. KITCHEN - NEXT DAY

The CAMERA pans across the morning kitchen to reveal Brandon
at the table eating a wide assortment of junk food. He is on
can number four of a six pack of coke.

He has the phone book out, the cordless phone on the table
and a jar full of quarters in front of him. He picks up the
phone and drops a quarter in the glass.

                    BRANDON
                (on the phone)
            Ah, yeah do you all ship bodies?
            ...Deceased bodies.

The party on the other end hangs up.

Ashley enters and goes to her coupon box on the wall and
files some coupons. She looks over at Brandon and his mess.
He gets up and gives her the jar of quarters.

                    BRANDON (cont'd)
            For the calls I made.

Brandon throws away his trash. He then picks up the four
empty coke cans and throws them in the trash. Ashley is
appalled. She goes in the trash can, gets them out and puts
them in another trash can marked 'Recycle Aluminum'.

She exits. Brandon stands dumbfounded.

EXT. SIDEWALK IN FRONT OF THE HOUSE - DAY

The mailman comes up to the house with a package and a few
pieces of mail. He RINGS the doorbell. Brandon answers the
door in his favorite tank top.

                    MAILMAN
            Mr. Bell, how are you today?

                    BRANDON
        Fine.

He hands Brandon a clipboard to sign for the package and
Brandon does.

                    MAILMAN
            How's the wife?

                    BRANDON
        She's doing fine.

The Mailman exits.

INSIDE THE HOUSE

Brandon sits down on the couch and places the package on the
coffee table. He thumbs through the mail and lays it on the
couch beside him. He opens the package and reveals a
camcorder. He pulls it out and starts to put it together.
Ashley comes out of her room, just waking up, wearing one of
Vernon's shirts and sweat pants.

                    ASHLEY
          Who were you talking to?

                    BRANDON
               (without looking up)
          Mailman.

                    ASHLEY
          Where's the mail?

                    BRANDON
          Right here.

She looks at the flap on the box and sees the address label
with Vernon's name on it as Brandon reads the instructions.

                    ASHLEY
          You opened Vernon's package? You
          shouldn't be opening his mail.

                    BRANDON
          He won't mind.

                    ASHLEY
          Where's the rest of the mail?

                    BRANDON
          I've got it.

                    ASHLEY
          May I have it?

                    BRANDON
               (still reading)
          After I've gone through it.

                    ASHLEY
               (incredulous at his
                audacity)
          What?!

He puts the instructions down and picks up the stack of mail.

> BRANDON
> I have a right to know what mail
> comes into this house.

He starts to sort through it. He raises up the first letter
and reads the outside.

> BRANDON (cont'd)
> Coupons!

He throws it on the floor. She snatches them up.

> ASHLEY
> (close to hysteria)
> You can't go through my mail!

> BRANDON
> (holding up another
> envelope)
> South Bay Hospital for Mr. & Mrs.
> Vernon Bell. It's got my brother's
> name on it so I can open it.

Ashley freaks out as he starts to open the letter. She
reaches for the mail several times but he holds it away from
her. She punches him hard on his bad arm, he slumps in
serious pain and drops the mail.

She snatches up the letter from the hospital and runs. He
chases her down the hall, but she dashes into her room, slams
and locks the door before he can catch her.

> BRANDON (cont'd)
> (frustrated)
> GOD DAMN IT!!

Still holding his arm, he kicks the door to release his
frustration.

ON THE OTHER SIDE OF THE DOOR

Ashley sits on the floor by the bed clutching the letter,
shaking with fear.

Brandon runs out of steam and walks off.

EXT. SUN SHINES THROUGH THE WINDOW - MORNING

Ashley awakes, rolls over and gets out of bed. She comes out
of her room and hears water running and Brandon brushing his
teeth. She stops and frowns.

Ashley walks up to his bathroom door and KNOCKS on it. He
opens the door, no shirt on, mouth filled with toothpaste and
brush and gives her a 'what do you want' look. She walks
into the bathroom, turns the water off and exits.

INT. GARAGE - LATER

The door opens and Brandon enters slowly. He walks up to the
Benz. He takes a deep breath and takes his time opening the
door. He peeks inside, sees the dried blood all over the
interior of the car, slams the door and goes back inside.

                                        DISSOLVE TO:

AN EXTENDED MONTAGE

EXT. BRANDON AT A BUS STOP - DAY

The RTD city bus comes down the street, stops, and Brandon
gets on board.

On the bus, Brandon pulls out his pen and pad. Before he can
begin writing he looks up just in time to see the bus go by
MCCORMICK MORTUARY. He makes a note to go back there later.

BRANDON GETS OFF ONE BUS

and transfers to another. Again he pulls out his notepad.

                    BRANDON (V.O.)
                (thinks)
            Black men... a dying breed.
                (scratches it out)
            Black men... an endangered species.

Brandon thinks but is still not satisfied with the opening.

THE MONTAGE CONTINUES WITH

BRANDON GETTING OFF THE BUS

and entering an office building.

INSIDE THE LAW OFFICES

Brandon stands in front of the RECEPTIONIST. She glances
over an appointment book before telling him to comeback at
another time. (MOS)

BRANDON BACK ON THE BUS

writing in his notepad.

> BRANDON (V.O.)
> Why are we killing ourselves?

He thinks about how to expand upon the opening.

BRANDON GETTING OFF THE BUS

in a residential section of Compton. He checks the address
on a wadded up piece of paper before walking up to the house
and knocking on the door.

Frustrated that no one is home he walks off.

STILL IN COMPTON

Brandon is knocking on another door. An ELDERLY WOMAN peeks
her head out of the door.

Brandon asks her a few questions MOS before she slams the
door in his face.

Brandon pounds on the door until he realizes he's not going
to get any cooperation from her and decides to move on.

A DIFFERENT HOUSE

and another door slammed in his face.

                                              CUT TO:

Brandon following a MAN down the street trying to ask him questions.

                                        CUT TO:

ANOTHER AND ANOTHER DOOR

slammed in his face continuing the montage.

BRANDON BACK AT THE LAW OFFICES

waiting impatiently in the outer office. He is attracting looks as the conservative types walk by him.

                                        CUT TO:

THE UCLA CAMPUS SIGN

Brandon walks by.

                                        CUT TO:

Him setting the video camera up on a tripod.

                                        CUT TO:

ONE OF VERNON'S FRIENDS

speaking in front of the video camera.

                    FIRST FRIEND
          I think we got along so well
          because he wasn't always trying to
          over exaggerate who he was. What I
          mean is some people feel that if
          they don't keep harping on it...
          you're gonna forget they're black.
          He wasn't like that.

                                        CUT TO:

BRANDON TAILING

A WOMAN down the street as he tries to ask her questions.

                                        CUT TO:

AN INTERVIEW

                    SECOND FRIEND
          Man, he was a cool dude. Man, I
          was totally bummed out when I heard
          the news, man. Wow!

                                        CUT BACK TO:

BRANDON AT THE LAW OFFICES

Waiting. THEO, a sharply dressed black attorney in his early
thirties, enters. He very friendly shakes Brandon's hand and
apologizes for the delay. (MOS)

EXT. LATE MODEL BMW

gliding through traffic with Theo behind the wheel and
Brandon on the passenger side.

                    THEO
          We were hired to assist the firm in
          dealing with minority cases.
          Vernon had a great winning streak.
          But they didn't always turn out
          favorable for the minority side.
          He didn't care, he just took the
          money and ran. He even went out,
          bought a brand new Benz and started
          giving money to the Republican
          party.

                    BRANDON
                 (disappointed)
          The Republicans?!

                    THEO
          Everybody knows real brothers are
          Democrats and drive Beemers.

INT. RESTAURANT LOBBY - LATER

The lobby is small but has lots of plants, windows and light.

Brandon and Theo enter. Theo blends in perfectly with the
predominantly white clientele. His necktie even matches the
table cloths.

Brandon sticks out like a sore thumb while Theo schmoozes
briefly with the Maitre'd and waves at a few people.

                                                    CUT TO:

INT. RESTAURANT - DINING ROOM - LATER

Theo attacks his salad as he tries to suppress his bitter
hostility toward Vernon.

                         THEO
               He began to speak out against
               affirmative action. Affirmative
               action got him hired. That's when
               the NAACP came after him.

                         BRANDON
               What happened?

Theo pauses with his salad.

                         THEO
               I thought I knew Vernon. Instead
               of him complying with the NAACP, he
               resigned and went to work for Legal
               Services.
                    (incredulous)
               Legal services! Why?

Theo seems to be just as confused and passionate about Vernon
as Brandon.

                         BRANDON
               Did you all stay in touch?

                         THEO
               I tried... He never wanted to talk
               about it.
                    (feels very betrayed)
               We used to be tight. He was my
               boy.
                    (beat)
               He didn't have to go out like that.

A sharply dressed BLACK MAN passes by the table holding hands
with a VOLUPTUOUS BLONDE. He smiles and nods to Theo on his
way by.

                         THEO (cont'd)
               He works in our entertainment
               division. Reminds me a lot of
               Vernon.
                    (more)

45.

                    THEO (cont'd)
          I'm always trying to rap to him
          about 'the experience' but he's
          just not with it.
                    (beat)
          What happens when brothers don't
          wanna be brothers anymore?

Theo returns to his salad.

                                        CUT TO:

BRANDON BACK ON THE BUS

holding his pad but staring out the window. Theo's words
echo in his mind.

                    THEO (V.O.)
          What happens when brothers don't
          wanna be brothers anymore?

THE MONTAGE INTENSIFIES

with A SERIES OF SHOTS WITH BRANDON transferring from bus to
bus. INTER-CUT WITH INTERVIEWS.

                    THIRD FRIEND
          Yeah, we worked at the Sloppy Dog
          together. He borrowed twenty
          dollars from me and never paid me
          back. I tried to call him, but
          they wouldn't put me through. Then
          I hear word that he's looking to
          pay me back. After all these
          years. I sho could use that money
          right about now. He didn't give it
          to you, did he?

                                        CUT TO:

BRANDON BACK AT A HOUSE IN COMPTON

He knocks on the door and is let in.

IN THE LIVING ROOM

MARY, an attractive African-American sister, with an up front
attitude, is picking up her messy home to accommodate her
unexpected guest.

                    MARY
          Brandon, come on in! It's good to
          see you!

Brandon is a little put off by her outward hospitality.

                    MARY (cont'd)
          I wish I had known you were coming.
          I would have cooked you dinner.
          You look great. Have a seat.

They sit on the couch.

                    BRANDON
          I'm not gonna stay long.

Mary slides closer to him.

                    MARY
          You know, it's a shame you ended up
          in prison. I always said you had
          it going on. So what's up?

                    BRANDON
          Just trying to get the 411 on
          Vernon.

                    MARY
               (she sighs heavily)
          Vernon.

Just the sound of his name stirs up an array of emotions in
Mary. Escaping the issue, Mary jumps up and heads for the
kitchen.

                    MARY (cont'd)
          You hungry?

                    BRANDON
          No.

                    MARY
          It won't take me long to whip
          something up.

Brandon follows her into the kitchen.

                    BRANDON
          Look, Mary, I didn't come to eat.
          Just tell me what you know.

Corners her.

                  MARY
               (defensive)
          I don't want to go there!

                BRANDON
         You hiding something?

                  MARY
     No.

In her face.

                BRANDON
         Why don't you want to talk?

She tries to move away but he grabs her. She breaks away and
explodes under pressure.

                  MARY
     Because your brother was a two-
     faced bastard!! That's why!!

Her outburst and assault has left him speechless.

                MARY (cont'd)
     He woke up one morning and decided
     sisters weren't good enough. If a
     brother feels like he's gotta play
     in the snow, then go the hell on.
     Just stay away from me.

                BRANDON
     Was he trying to come back?

                  MARY
               (laughs)
     He'd call me and give me this jazz
     about how he would come visit me
     but he was afraid. He said someone
     might break into his Benz. I said
     "Fuck you and your Benz!"

                BRANDON
     He lived here!

                  MARY
     After the shit he pulled, he had
     every right to be afraid to show
     his ass in the hood.

Mary sees that Brandon is upset by his brother's behavior.
She tries to comfort him.

                        MARY (cont'd)
          Let me heat up some neck bones and
          gravy for you.

                        BRANDON
          No, I gotta go.

Brandon exits.

BACK ON THE BUS

Brandon writes feverishly in his notepad. He is very
restless and upset with what he's heard about Vernon. As his
inner dialogue continues his anger swells. Outraged, he
screams and punches the back of the seat. All the PEOPLE ON
THE BUS turn and look at him.

                                        CUT TO:

AN INTERVIEW

                        FOURTH FRIEND
          My wife and Ashley used to temp
          together. You never saw a happier
          couple. I don't understand why the
          NAACP had to come down so hard on
          him.

EXT. BUS - LATER

The bus stops at the corner. Brandon is among the passengers
getting off the bus. He crosses the street and enters The
McCormick Mortuary.

INT. MORTUARY - MOMENTS LATER

Brandon enters and is greeted by FRANK, the mortician. They
shake hands and he escorts Brandon to

THE BACK ROOM

As Brandon views the body, a thread of tension runs through
his face. He takes a couple of deep breaths to endure the
grief but has to turn away. Frank steps in and conceals the
body.

                    FRANK
          I understand how your family feels.
          But the Krutzers are awfully nice
          people and have spared no expense.

Brandon is still trying to regain his strength.

                    FRANK (CONT'D) (cont'd)
          I wouldn't suggest moving the body
          that far. Maybe if you'd come a
          day earlier. The expense and
          hassle would be a disservice to the
          deceased.

OUTSIDE THE MORTUARY

Obviously weak from viewing the body, Brandon staggers down
the street trying to remain unaffected but the pain hits him,
forces him down onto the curb and into tears.

An LAPD patrol car drives by and slows down. The OFFICER
flips his siren on and off. Brandon looks up, the Officer
points to a 'NO LOITERING' sign. Brandon composes himself,
gets up and moves on.

BRANDON ON THE BUS

Slouched down in his seat, Brandon's weary eyes stare blankly
out the window oblivious to the other African-American and
Latino faces on the bus. He pulls out his notepad.

                    BRANDON (V.O.)
               (big sigh)
          Black men...
               (pause)
          ... confused.

EXT. CITY BUS - EVENING

The bus comes to a stop and Brandon gets off and walks up the
hill toward the house.

He gets to the house, grabs the mail out of the box and
enters the house ENDING THE MONTAGE.

INT. LIVING ROOM - SAME

Brandon looks around to see if Ashley is there but sees no
signs of her. He goes into his room and drops the camcorder
and the mail on the floor.

The doorbell RINGS.

Brandon moves to the living room and opens the door. It's
Tom.

                    BRANDON
          What?

                    TOM
          Is... is Ashley home?

                    BRANDON
          No!

                    TOM
          I just wanted to say hi. I'll come
          back later.

                    BRANDON
          Yeah, like next year.

Brandon slams the door.

                    BRANDON (cont'd)
          Damn, he ain't even in the ground
          and the dogs have already arrived.

Brandon proceeds down the hall. He stops in front of
Ashley's closed bedroom door. He thinks maybe he shouldn't
go in, but he does.

He looks through a few drawers before going into the walk-in
closet. Brandon looks at all of Vernon's nice suits. He
searches through some shoe boxes on the top shelf and finds a
box of pictures and letters. All the pictures are snapshots
of Ashley by herself. He puts the letters in his pocket and
puts the shoe box back.

He turns to Ashley's side of the closet and goes through her
things until he finds a decorative box with letters in it.
He opens it and pulls out a letter from Vernon to her and
reads it.

                    BRANDON (V.O.) (cont'd)
          My Sweet Ashley, I hope you are
          having a wonderful time in Hawaii.
                    (more)

                    BRANDON (V.O.) (cont'd)
          Mitch and I have been hanging out
          together. He's pretty cool.

Brandon scans the letter and moves on to the next page before
something of interest catches his eye.

                    BRANDON (V.O.) (cont'd)
          I'm going to write Brandon and find
          out when his parole begins.
          Hopefully he'll be out in time for
          the wedding. I'd like to have at
          least one member of my family
          there. They'd like you if they got
          to know you.

Brandon hears the front door open and he freezes.

INT. LIVING ROOM - SAME

Ashley enters with her outspoken friend CAROL.

                    CAROL
          I want to meet him. You know I
          always regretted not keeping Vernon
          for myself. If he looks anything
          like Vernon--

                    ASHLEY
          Carol, calm down. I don't think
          he's even here.

Carol sits in the living room and Ashley KNOCKS on Brandon's
door.

                                        CUT TO:

Brandon hiding in Ashley's closet, listening to her knock on
his door.

                    ASHLEY (cont'd)
          He's not here.

Brandon starts to come out.

                    ASHLEY (cont'd)
          Let me get out of these shoes.

Carol picks up a copy of Brandon's newspaper, The Radical
View, and flips through it. Ashley goes in her bedroom. She
pauses when she sees the door open. She kicks her shoes off
in the middle of the floor.

Ashley starts toward the closet but gets dizzy and stops.
She backs up and sits down on the bed for a second. She then
gets up and enters the closet, grabs her house shoes, slips
them on and exits. She closes the bedroom door behind her.

Brandon steps out of the tub from behind the shower curtain.
He is on his way out when he hears Carol.

> CAROL
> So, Ashley, why do you think he did
> it?

Brandon listens attentively. Before Ashley can answer Carol
interrupts her.

> CAROL (cont'd)
> (still flipping through
> the paper)
> What is this garbage?

> ASHLEY
> Oh, that's his.

> CAROL
> (drops the paper)
> So, what's he like? Is he cute?

> ASHLEY
> He's all right. He's shorter than
> Vernon.

Brandon frowns at her assessment of him. Ashley sits on the
couch.

> CAROL
> You know I'm not the type to go out
> with one of them. I mean, what
> would our sorority sisters think?
> Well I know what they would think.
> But who cares, we've outgrown that
> sorority scene, haven't we, Ashley?
> Anyway it's been so long since I've
> had a real man, I'll take whatever
> I can get.
> (fakes a laugh)
> I'm kidding, Ashley. Is he gonna
> be home soon? What's he like?

> ASHLEY
> I can't figure him out. I've never
> met anyone who can talk like a
> Harvard graduate and a truck driver
> from one sentence to the next.
> (more)

                    ASHLEY (cont'd)
          I guess that's what a prison degree
          will give you. Sometimes he's just
          downright crude.

Again Brandon is displeased by what he hears.

                    CAROL
          Sometimes the crude ones make the
          best lovers.

                    ASHLEY
          Vernon was no slouch in that
          department.

                    CAROL
          Oh really now?

Ashley gets up to go in the kitchen and feels another dizzy
spell coming on and sits back down.

                    CAROL (cont'd)
          Ashley...

                    ASHLEY
          I shouldn't have gone shopping.

                    CAROL
          But shopping has always made you
          feel better. Remember when you
          flunked chemistry, what did we do
          to cheer you up? Remember when you
          had that yeast infection... Come
          on, let's go out for a drink.
          You'll feel much better.

                    ASHLEY
          Carol, come on.

                    CAROL
          Okay, okay, take your time and
          whenever you're ready we're gonna
          go out and find you another man!
          Because you used to be very popular
          with the guys. You had a wonderful
          single life.

                    ASHLEY
          I remember being hurt a lot.

                    CAROL
          A lot of good looking white men
          said they had written you off, but
          now that you are single again ...
                    (more)

>   CAROL (cont'd)
>   Unless it is true what they say.
>   Once you go black ...

Carol looks at Ashley but she refuses to respond to Carol's
implication.

>   ASHLEY
>   I'll never go back to jerks.

>   CAROL
>   I hate to inform you but that's all
>   that's out there.

Carol exits to the bathroom.

Ashley goes into the kitchen and pulls some vegetables out of
the refrigerator. She bends over to get a pot out of a lower
cabinet, raises up and is scared by Brandon standing in the
doorway.

>   ASHLEY
>   (upset)
>   Do you have to sneak up on me like
>   that?!

She slams the pot down on the stove.

>   ASHLEY (cont'd)
>   Don't you have something to do?
>   Some place to go?

>   BRANDON
>   I've already been everywhere today.
>   I even went to see some of your
>   friends. Now it's your turn to
>   answer some questions.

Brandon watches her vent her frustration as she cuts up her
vegetables improperly using a French knife.

>   ASHLEY
>   I didn't give you permission to
>   harass my friends.

Carol enters.

>   CAROL
>   I'm one of her friends you can
>   harass.

Brandon turns and looks her up and down. He then looks away
as if to say 'No Thank You'.

                          CAROL (cont'd)
          Don't give me that look. We can
          cut to the chase.

                          BRANDON
          Let's cut to the chase. I'm not
          like my brother. I don't do snow
          bunnies.

Ashley gestures with the knife.

                          ASHLEY
          I will not have you insulting my
          friends in my house.

                          CAROL
          I heard you were in prison. Is it
          true you actually killed a man?
          How did you do it? With a gun, a
          knife or with your bare hands? And
          why? What made you kill him?

                          BRANDON
          He kept asking me stupid questions.

                          CAROL
          Vernon sure was a hell of a lot
          friendlier.
                    (moving on)
          Ashley, do you need a ride to the
          lawyer's office tomorrow?

                          ASHLEY
          No thanks.

                          CAROL
          When are you gonna get another car?

                          ASHLEY
          We were in the process of finding
          me one. I haven't been able to
          clean up his. Let alone go in the
          garage.

                          CAROL
          All right, you take care. And
          don't let this ogre get on your
          nerves. If you need me, call me,
          okay, Honey?

They hug and kiss each other on the cheek.

                         ASHLEY
              Okay.

Carol gives Brandon a quick glance over as she walks by.

                         BRANDON
              Okay, let's talk, Mrs. Bell. Or
              should I say Ms. Krutzer. Since
              you'll be going back to your maiden
              name now that you are a free woman
              again. That's probably why you're
              going to see your lawyer.

                         ASHLEY
              For your information, I'm going to
              hear Vernon's will read. And
              before you even say it, you are
              invited.

                         BRANDON
              I better be.

                         ASHLEY
              You are. Now leave me alone. Go
              to your room, do something. Just
              get out of my sight.

                         BRANDON
              You're going to have to talk to me
              sooner or later.

Ashley begins to lose her temper as she continues cutting the
vegetables.

                         ASHLEY
              Not if you keep badgering me! You
              come waltzing in here like you're
              the only person who's lost
              something!

Ashley continues working the knife vigorously and releasing
her emotions more to herself than directly at him.

                         ASHLEY (cont'd)
              You cut him out of your life but he
              was still very much a part of mine.
              Vernon was my husband, I loved him
              and I miss him!! I was the one who
              saw him every morning when I woke
              up and cuddled next to him every
              night before I went to sleep!
                         (more)

> ASHLEY (cont'd)
> And now I can't do that because
> he's gone! AND I DON'T HAVE ANY
> ANSWERS EITHER!!!

Ashley brings the knife down and slices her finger wide open.

> ASHLEY (cont'd)
> Damn it!!

She grabs her finger and blood goes everywhere. Brandon
doesn't know how to react.

> ASHLEY (cont'd)
> (in pain)
> Look at what you made me do!!

She squeezes her hand as the blood pours out.

> BRANDON
> Run some cold water over it.

Ashley just stands there with her eyes closed and squeezing
her hand.

> BRANDON (cont'd)
> Run some water over it!! I'll get
> you a Band-aid.

As Brandon turns to exit, she faints. He rushes to her aid
on the kitchen floor.

EXT. CITY STREETS - NIGHT

An ambulance races through the city.

INT. EMERGENCY ROOM WAITING AREA - LATER

The DOCTOR comes up to Brandon sitting on the couch. Brandon
stands up.

> FIRST DOCTOR
> Mr. Bell?

> BRANDON
> Uh... yeah.

> FIRST DOCTOR
> She cut her finger pretty badly but
> she's going to be fine. And she
> was having those dizzy spells
> because, well... Your wife is
> pregnant.

                    BRANDON
                  (shocked)
          Oh shit.

INT. LIVING ROOM - LATER THAT NIGHT

Brandon and Ashley enter.

                    BRANDON
          How come you didn't tell me you
          were pregnant?

                    ASHLEY
          Because I didn't.

                    BRANDON
          You should have told me.

                    ASHLEY
          Why, are you a doctor?

Not having to stick around for the answer, Ashley goes in her
room and closes her door.

EXT. PALM TREE ON A CLOUDY, HAZY CALI DAY - AM

INT. GARAGE - SAME

The CAMERA slowly moves from the back of the Benz to the
front as the sound of scrubbing is heard. Brandon has the
front door open with a bucket of soap and water as he scrubs
the blood out of the front seat interior.

A very painful experience for him, he stops to try and regain
his composure.

                    BRANDON (V.O.)
          This shit's not coming out. If
          people could see how big of a mess
          they leave behind...
                  (throws the sponge down)
          Maybe he was afraid of bringing a
          racially mixed child into the
          world.

Brandon goes in the house.

INT. LIVING ROOM - MOMENTS LATER

Ashley comes out of the bedroom putting on her earrings.
Brandon is sprawled out on the couch in a depressed state.

                    ASHLEY
          Okay, I'm dressed.

                    BRANDON
               (sits up)
          I was hoping we could take his
          car...

Ashley tenses up.

                    ASHLEY
          No. I'm not ready yet.

They share a mutual feeling of grief.

EXT. BUS STOP - DAY

Brandon is sitting on the back of the bench with his feet on
the seat. Ashley is standing in front of the bench.

                    BRANDON
          You should be sitting down.

                    ASHLEY
          Why?

                    BRANDON
          You're pregnant. You should stay
          off your feet.

                    ASHLEY
          Oh, you are a doctor.

Brandon sighs heavily because once again she's gotten the
best of him.

INT. LAWYER'S OFFICE - DAY

HAROLD, the attorney, is seated behind his desk with papers
before him. Ashley and Brandon sit across from him.

                    HAROLD
          Now what I usually like to do is go
          back and review the distribution of
          assets.
               (more)

> HAROLD (cont'd)
> To put everything in layman's terms
> just to make sure all parties
> understand what's going on. How
> does that sound?

Ashley and Brandon nod.

> HAROLD (cont'd)
> The house, and I think this was
> pretty clear, goes to Ashley.
> Fifty percent of all of his liquid
> assets, what's in his checking
> account, goes to Ashley. The
> remainder is to be set up in a
> trust fund for his first born
> child. And Brandon, you will
> receive his financial portfolio.

> BRANDON
> His what?

> HAROLD
> His investments. You know, stocks,
> bonds, and CDs. It should be worth
> quite a bit. The exact value will
> be appraised at a later date. It
> will be several months before you
> receive anything because of all the
> legal proceedings. And that's it
> for the major assets. Brandon,
> your brother was a smart man. He
> left everything in order.

Harold picks up a sealed envelope.

> HAROLD (cont'd)
> Also, this is a letter he included
> in here for you, Ashley, just last
> week.

He hands her the letter. She opens it and it's a short note
on a single page. She reads it while the men are silent.
She lowers the letter and starts to weep.

Brandon is uncomfortable and wants to help but doesn't know
what to do. Harold hands Brandon a box of tissues. He takes
them and gives one to Ashley.

> HAROLD (cont'd)
> Oh, and there's one other thing
> here.
> (more)

> HAROLD (cont'd)
> He states that he wishes to be
> buried in his wife's family plot,
> because, I quote here, "The
> Krutzers have been very supportive
> and accepted me wholly, spiritually
> and without prejudgment."
> (he closes the file)
> Any questions?

INT. LOBBY OF THE OFFICE BUILDING - MINUTES LATER

Brandon and Ashley are on their way out of the building. He
is babbling to try and lighten the moment.

> BRANDON
> I always thought a portfolio was
> something a model used to carry
> pictures in. I always thought CDs
> were music. Why did he have to
> leave me that? Was he pissed off
> at me? I was hoping he'd leave me
> some cash.
> (beat)
> You wanna trade?

EXT. SMALL OUTDOOR CAFE - DAY

Brandon and Ashley sit at a table. She watches him eat
everything with his fingers and then lick his fingers.

> ASHLEY
> You know, they've invented these
> wonderful things called a fork and
> a napkin.

He gives her a dirty look, but wipes his hands on his napkin,
picks up his fork and uses it.

There is an awkward moment of silence between them. Ashley
knows she's won the battle of the burial but she wants to be
understanding.

> ASHLEY (cont'd)
> Maybe your parents could come out.

> BRANDON
> They don't believe in airplanes.

EXT. ASHLEY'S HOUSE - NIGHT

INT. LIVING ROOM - SAME

Brandon on the couch labeling and logging video tapes.

INT. WALK-IN CLOSET - SAME

Ashley packs Vernon's clothes in a suitcase. She closes the
case and exits.

Ashley enters the living room with the suitcase. She sets it
down beside Brandon.

                    ASHLEY
          I want you to have these.

Ashley opens the suitcase and begins laying the clothes out
all over the living room as if preparing for a fashion show.

                    BRANDON
          I've got clothes.

                    ASHLEY
          Everything you own has a hood on
          it. What are you, a monk? In
          California you have to wear things
          that have personality.

                    BRANDON
          But I'm leaving.

                    ASHLEY
          Well you're going out in style.

                    BRANDON
          Ever heard that saying "clothes
          don't make the man"?

                    ASHLEY
          Whoever said that didn't know how
          to shop.
              (excited)
          Now I bought this shirt for him
          when we were in San Francisco.

She holds it up next to him.

                    BRANDON
          I ain't wearing nothing from San
          Francisco. I'd get kicked out of
          the 'hood.

                         ASHLEY
          How are they going to know?

                         BRANDON
          They'll be able to look at it and
          tell.
                    (mimics his friends)
          Yo, man, look at that shirt Brandon
          got on! Where he get that shit
          from, Frisco?

                         ASHLEY
          You shouldn't worry about what
          other people think. Now stop being
          such a fuddie duddie and try it on.

                         BRANDON
          I'm not wearing my brother's
          clothes.

                         ASHLEY
          He won't mind.

                         BRANDON
          Nope, can't do it.

                         ASHLEY
                    (frustrated)
          Just take them! You don't have to
          wear them, just take them for me!
                    (releasing the truth of
                    her objective)
          I can't throw them away or give
          them to some stranger. But if you
          don't want to, you don't have to.

She picks up the clothes and stuffs them back in the
suitcase.

                         BRANDON
                    (finally sympathetic)
          I'll take them.

                         ASHLEY
                    (relieved)
          Thanks.

EXT. ASHLEY'S HOUSE - NIGHT

Tom walks up to the front door with a coffee cup in his hand
and stops. He takes a deep breath and releases a big sigh.

                   TOM
                (rehearsing)
        Hello... Hi... Hey... How's it
        going?

Still unsure of his approach, he mumbles through a few
rehearsals.

                   TOM (cont'd)
                (sighs heavily)
        You got it? Yeah, I think so.

He RINGS the doorbell. While waiting for an answer he
rehearses a few more times. Ashley opens the door.

                   ASHLEY
                (surprised)
        Tom, how are you? Come on in.

He enters. Brandon watches them from the kitchen.

                   TOM
                (nervous)
        Fine. I'm fine.

                   ASHLEY
        I haven't seen you around in a
        while. You been doing okay?

                   TOM
        Yeah. I came to borrow a cup.

                   ASHLEY
        A cup?

                   TOM
        Yeah, a cup.
                (beat)
        I want to have some coffee.

                   ASHLEY
        You have a cup in your hand.

                   TOM
                (realizes his mistake)
        I meant a cup of sugar. A cup of
        sugar.

Ashley smiles at his humbleness. From the kitchen Brandon
shakes his head in disgust at Tom's behavior around Ashley.

                    ASHLEY
          Sure, you can have the whole bag.
          I wasn't the one who ate refined
          sugar around here.

They move to the kitchen. Tom is startled when he sees
Brandon.

                    ASHLEY (cont'd)
          He likes scaring people. This is
          Vernon's brother Brandon.

                    TOM
               (trying to loosen up)
          I actually thought you were...

                    ASHLEY
          And he likes pretending he's
          someone he's not.

Ashley hands Tom the sugar. The phone RINGS and Ashley exits
to answer it. Brandon stares at Tom long enough to make him
uncomfortable. He tries to make small talk.

                    TOM
          So, you here for the funeral?

Brandon doesn't answer but Tom doesn't give up.

                    TOM (cont'd)
          It's a shame. One day he's out
          working in the yard... next day...
          blam! What made him do it?

                    BRANDON
          He knew the guy down the street was
          gonna move in on his territory and
          he didn't think he could compete.

Tom is speechless.

                    BRANDON (cont'd)
          Borrow a cup of sugar. She saw
          right through that weak shit.

Tom looks stupid and unable to think of what to say.

                    BRANDON (cont'd)
          What do you see in her?

                    TOM
          The same thing Vernon saw in her.
          She's pretty and she's nice.

                    BRANDON
          But she's white. Don't you know
          any sisters?

Tom wants to avoid confrontation.

                    TOM
          I'll go now.

                    BRANDON
          Yeah, you're dismissed.

Brandon watches Tom exit with his tail between his legs.

                    BRANDON (cont'd)
               (shakes his head)
          Poor excuse for a brother.

Ashley re-enters and sees Tom is gone.

                    ASHLEY
          Where did Tom go?

                    BRANDON
          Who was that on the phone?

                    ASHLEY
          You mean you don't have the lines
          bugged?

Brandon gives Ashley a 'that's real funny' look.

                    ASHLEY (cont'd)
          A guy I called about selling his
          car. Vernon and I were supposed to
          go look at it tomorrow. You wanna
          come?

EXT. DRIVEWAY - DAY

A used Volkswagen Golf is parked in a driveway with a 'For
Sale' sign in the window. Brandon walks around examining the
car.

Ashley is standing on the porch, talking to SHERWOOD, a
somewhat suspicious, cheesy man in his late thirties.

Because Sherwood seems to be beyond the sales pitch and
moving closer into Ashley, Brandon occasionally cuts his eyes
over at them.

Sherwood goes to touch Ashley and she backs off. Brandon
comes over.

                    BRANDON
          Ashley, let's go.

                    SHERWOOD
          We're discussing business.

                    BRANDON
          Now, Ashley.

                    SHERWOOD
               (turns ugly)
          Buddy, you got some nerve
          interfering with my business deal.
          You know I could shoot your ass
          just for being on my property.

Unafraid, Brandon takes a few steps forward.

                    BRANDON
          Well, you better kill me.

Ashley throws herself in front of Brandon and starts pushing
him backwards.

                    ASHLEY
          Okay, let's go.

Brandon resists as she pushes him off Sherwood's property and
down the street.

EXT. CITY STREET - MOMENTS LATER

Brandon and Ashley walking down the street. She is furious.

                    ASHLEY
          You can't solve everything with
          violence!

                    BRANDON
          And you can't always give people
          the benefit of the doubt. You just
          can't.

Ashley sees that Brandon is getting worked up.

                    ASHLEY
          When did you become so concerned
          about me?

>   BRANDON
>   It's not for you. Any stupid
>   decisions you make affect my
>   nephew.

She is pleasantly surprised by his comment.

>   ASHLEY
>   How do you know I'm going to have a
>   boy?

Brandon doesn't want to drop his guard.

>   BRANDON
>   Look, if you're going to spend that
>   kind of money, you should look at
>   something new. You can trade
>   Vernon's in and get two cars.

EXT. MONTAGE OF NEW CARS - DAY

Brandon and Ashley on car lot after car lot test driving an
array of cars. The following conversations are heard over
the visuals of them car shopping.

>   ASHLEY (V.O.)
>   And I read that nonsense you wrote
>   in that paper. The white man is
>   not responsible for all poverty and
>   oppression in America. And Vernon
>   would agree with me.

>   BRANDON (V.O.)
>   He has all the jobs and the power
>   to create government programs to
>   help people rise out of poverty.
>   Because they can't do it alone.

Ashley and Brandon on a different car lot.

>   BRANDON (V.O.) (cont'd)
>   What do you mean you all never
>   talked about it? You were an inter-
>   racial couple. What else was there
>   to talk about besides racism.

>   ASHLEY (V.O.)
>   We never saw each other as
>   different. We chose to acknowledge
>   more of our similarities than our
>   differences.
>   (more)

                    ASHLEY (V.O.) (cont'd)
          Him graduating from UCLA and me
          from USC was a much bigger issue.

Brandon and Ashley on yet another car lot.

                    BRANDON (V.O.)
                 (incredulous)
          Is your birthday really April 22nd?

                    ASHLEY (V.O.)
          Is your birthday really April 22nd?

                    BRANDON (V.O.)
          It sure is.

                    ASHLEY (V.O.)
          So is mine.

                    BRANDON (V.O.)
          I knew there was some reason why I
          hated you before I even met you.

                    ASHLEY (V.O.)
          I knew there was some reason why I
          hated you even after I met you.

INT. LIVING ROOM - NIGHT

Brandon and Ashley are collapsed on the couch. She massages
her feet.

                    BRANDON
          Hate is a very strong word.

                    ASHLEY
          Well, I dislike you, then.

                    BRANDON
          Dislike. Just don't use hate.
          Hate is a powerful emotion and you
          have no reason to hate.

                    ASHLEY
          Okay, I dislike you, Brandon, how's
          that?

                    BRANDON
          Yeah, that'll work.

                    ASHLEY
          That'll work. Vernon used to say
          that all the time.

                         BRANDON
               He got it from me.

Pause.

                         ASHLEY
               But you hate me, don't you?

                         BRANDON
               Yeap.

                         ASHLEY
               Thought so.
                    (pause)
               So, you talked to your parents
               lately?

                         BRANDON
               Nope.

                         ASHLEY
               They don't know the funeral's going
               to be here?

Brandon doesn't answer.

                         ASHLEY(cont'd)
               You'd better call them.
                    (she gets up)
               I'm going to bed.

                         BRANDON
               Is it okay if I use the phone?

                         ASHLEY
               No, you may not.
                    (beat)
               Of course you can.

                         BRANDON
               Seriously, my folks won't accept
               the charges.

                         ASHLEY
               I'll pay for the call. Goodnight.

She exits.

INT. BRANDON'S BEDROOM - LATER SAME NIGHT

Brandon enters, pushes his clothes off the bed and onto the
floor. The clothes cover a stack of unopened mail on the
floor.

He sits on the bed and stares at the phone. Brandon tries to
gather his courage before calling his parents. He finally
picks up the phone and dials.

> BRANDON
> Hey, Dad. It's me...She's paying
> for the call...Hey, you're going to
> be a grandfather...No, not the
> doctor, I just met her....Wait a
> sec, stop cross examining me. I'm
> not having a kid.
> (silence)
> Hello...Of course I'm sure...Well,
> you'd better have something to do
> with this mixed baby because it has
> your blood...
> (silence)
> No...Because in his will he
> requested to be buried here... The
> undertaker said it was too late. I
> wish you all could come out here...
> You could get killed in a car...
> This is your son... Don't call her
> that...I know Mama's upset...
> Well, then just wire me the money
> so I can come home then.
> (getting upset)
> HOW AM I SUPPOSED TO GET HOME?!!!

ASHLEY'S BEDROOM

Lying in bed, Ashley hears Brandon shouting.

> BRANDON (O.S.)
> Nah, you're crazy, we didn't make
> no deal!! What do you want me to
> do, strap his body to my back, drag
> him on the plane and say he's
> asleep?...I'm not being
> disrespectful!
> (lowering his voice)
> ... Tell me how I'm supposed to get
> back to Atlanta, walk?... Fine,
> I'll get the money my-damn-self!

BRANDON'S ROOM

Brandon slams the phone down, grabs his coat and cap and storms out the front door.

INT. HENRY BELL'S LIVING ROOM - SAME

He stands holding the phone, shocked that Brandon hung up on him. Clarice is standing in the doorway behind him. Henry finally hangs up the phone.

> CLARICE
> She's going to have Vernon's baby?

> HENRY
> That's what she's got him believing. Who knows what kinda lies she'll tell to get his insurance money. She don't fool me...

> CLARICE
> (upset)
> Henry, stop it! I can't take it anymore. I've let you talk me out of a lot of things. I even let you stop me from going to the wedding. You can't stop me from accepting my grandchild.

Henry stands rigid, unable to answer her.

> CLARICE (cont'd)
> You go on being a stubborn and bitter old man. I'm gonna be a grandparent.

She turns and exits leaving Henry standing alone and ashamed.

EXT. FRONT YARD - DAY

Ashley and Brandon watch a tow truck pull Vernon's Benz out of the garage and down the street. Brandon uses the remote and closes the garage door.

EXT. CEMETERY - DAY

A long shot of a small group of people standing on the hill around a gravesite. Brandon is the only black person attending his brother's funeral.

Ashley's PARENTS, her brother Mitch, and a few other friends
have come to pay their respects. They watch in silence as
the casket is lowered into the ground. Everyone starts to
walk away except Brandon and Ashley. He walks off, stops and
goes back for her.

EXT. DRIVEWAY - NIGHT

Ashley pulls up in her brand new Volkswagen Jetta.

Brandon picks up the garage door opener and presses the
button. The door is halfway up when Ashley takes it from
him, lowers the door and puts the remote in the glove
compartment. Ashley gets out of the car and enters the
house.

INT. LIVING ROOM - SAME NIGHT

Brandon is on the couch writing. Ashley is in the kitchen
cooking. They are still emotionally sedate from the funeral.
The house is quiet. Ashley comes to the entrance of the
living room, drying her hands.

                    ASHLEY
          Do you write all the time?

                    BRANDON
          Yep. I enjoy it.

                    ASHLEY
          Must be nice. I wanted to be a
          journalist but couldn't get past
          the writing part.

                    BRANDON
          Writing is good for the soul.

                    ASHLEY
              (beat)
          I'm going up to Santa Barbara to
          visit my parents tomorrow. You're
          welcome to come along.

Silence. Ashley comes into the living room and looks through
a shelf of CDs.

                    ASHLEY (cont'd)
          It's too quiet in here. Will I
          disturb you if I put on some music?

                    BRANDON
          You will if you put on Conway
          Twitty or "Achy Breaky Heart."

                    ASHLEY
                 (offended)
          Vernon taught me a lot about music.

She pops in a compact disc. Some nice, romantic R&B music
fills the living room. Brandon immediately recognizes the
tune and looks up. He is visually surprised by her
selection.

                    ASHLEY (cont'd)
                 (proud)
          I listen to classic old school.
          Babyface, Frankie Beverly and Maze,
          Luther Vandross...I even listen to
          rap.

                    BRANDON
          Yeah, "Rappers Delight."

Ashley really wants to impress him with her musical
knowledge.

                    ASHLEY
          No, old school rap.

                    BRANDON
          DJ Jazzy Jeff and the Fresh Prince.

                    ASHLEY
          Give me a break. I listen to P.E.

                    BRANDON
                 (shocked)
          Get the hell out of here!!! What
          do you know about Public Enemy?

                    ASHLEY
          I know all about Chuck D., Flavor
          Flav, Terminator X. They my house
          boys.

                    BRANDON
                 (correcting her)
          Homeboys. I can't believe you
          listen to P.E.

                    ASHLEY
          But I'd ask Vernon questions about
          what they were saying and he would
          laugh.

                    BRANDON
          Maybe he couldn't answer them
          himself.

                    ASHLEY
          There were a lot of things I wanted
          to know that he wouldn't answer.
          And not just with music.
                    (pause)
          I feel... Well...
                    (she dismisses her
                     thoughts)
          Well, never mind.

She starts to leave.

                    BRANDON
          What do you feel?

She reluctantly returns.

                    ASHLEY
          I feel...guilty. And I know you've
          been accusing me all along but it's
          a different kind of guilt. If I
          had been more in touch with....
          what do you call it? His
          'blackness.' I could have helped
          him through all this.

Brandon sees her turmoil but doesn't allow her to accept the
blame.

                    BRANDON
          Ashley...

Ashley gets up.

                    ASHLEY
                    (upset)
          I could have helped. I was his
          wife.

                    BRANDON
          You need to watch these tapes.

                        ASHLEY
                   (thinks a moment)
              I'd rather not.

She returns to the kitchen.

EXT. SANTA BARBARA BEACH HOUSE PATIO - DAY

Several people are on the patio deck overlooking the beach.
Ashley is off by herself.

Brandon and Mitch are nearby playing a friendly one on one
game of basketball.

LATER ON

Brandon eats lobster and ribs with a three-year-old LITTLE
GIRL. He entertains the little girl by playing silly games
with the food. Her face is covered with barbecue sauce.

Mitch walks over to a very pensive Ashley.

                        MITCH
              You still with us?

                        ASHLEY
              Yeah.

                        MITCH
              Hey, I'm glad you brought Brandon.

                        ASHLEY
              I remember the last time I left a
              man alone in my house.

                        MITCH
              He seems to be pretty well
              adjusted.

                        ASHLEY
              Are you kidding? He's very
              insecure.

                        MITCH
              I think he's enjoying himself, but
              he won't admit it. Looks like he's
              even made a new friend.

They look over and see him wiping the barbecue sauce off of
her hands and mouth as her MOTHER comes and gets her. She
thanks Brandon for baby-sitting. Brandon joins Ashley and
Mitch.

                    MITCH (cont'd)
          We were just talking about you.

                    BRANDON
          Why, is something missing?

                    MITCH
                 (laughs)
          You wanna take a walk?

                    BRANDON
          Yeah.

EXT. BEACH - MOMENTS LATER

Mitch and Brandon walk along the beach. Brandon throws rocks
into the ocean.

                    MITCH
          I'll be the first one to admit all
          I know about the 'black experience'
          I learned during the early sixties
          with the March on Washington. I
          was glad when King Day was
          acknowledged but that's about it
          for me.

                    BRANDON
          Yeah, you and the rest of white
          America. The March on Washington
          was not the end to end all.

                    MITCH
          But a lot of good came out of it.
                 (beat)
          I spent a great deal of time with
          Vernon. I took him to parties,
          introduced him to some of my
          buddies... Everyone was very
          impressed with him.
                 (he stops)
          Vernon was living proof of a man
          being judged by his character and
          not by the color of his skin. Is
          that not what the dream is all
          about?

Mitch studies Brandon for a reply. Brandon continues
throwing rocks as he thinks about what Mitch has just said.

                    BRANDON
          That sounds beautiful out here on
          the beach. But where I come from,
          that ain't how it goes down.

                    MITCH
               (after a moment of
               silence)
          Ashley tells me you've decided to
          stay for a while.

                    BRANDON
          I've still got some questions that
          need answering.

                    MITCH
          Ashley's been under a lot of stress
          lately.

                    BRANDON
               (defensive)
          So have I.

                    MITCH
               (sticking to his mission)
          Anything you can do to make things
          a little easier on her, I would
          appreciate.

After a moment.

                    MITCH (cont'd)
          You didn't have to let me win.

                    BRANDON
          I didn't want you to have me
          arrested.

EXT. FRONT OF ASHLEY'S HOUSE - LATER SAME NIGHT

Back in Palos Verdes.

INT. KITCHEN TABLE - SAME

Brandon and Ashley are seated at the table silently picking
over their half-eaten food.

                    ASHLEY
          How was it?

> BRANDON
> It was good. For white food.

> ASHLEY
> What did Mitch say to you?

> BRANDON
> He said if you got out of line I
> have permission to slap you upside
> the head.

Ashley chuckles at the absurdity.

Brandon gets up, grabs her plate and starts to clear the
table. Ashley starts to help but he gestures her away.

Ashley thinks this is too good to be true but decides not to
look a gift horse in the mouth.

She pulls up a bar stool and watches him work.

> ASHLEY
> (a fond memory)
> Vernon loved cooking. He used to
> surprise me with a weekend feast.
> On Saturday we would have breakfast
> in bed and then he'd grill that
> afternoon. Baby back ribs, corn on
> the cob, umm um! Then he'd make
> the best peach cobbler. Then we'd
> sleep late on Sunday and he'd take
> me out to a champagne brunch. Then
> we'd end with a nice candlelight
> dinner at home.

Brandon is now loading the dishwasher.

> BRANDON
> I didn't think you California
> people ate like that.

> ASHLEY
> We don't. That was Vernon's
> southern roots coming through.
> Feeding me was one of his ways of
> saying I love you. Of course
> that's why I'm so fat now.

Brandon checks out her slim figure.

> BRANDON
> You're not fat.

                    ASHLEY
          Yes I am. I need to lose five
          pounds.

                    BRANDON
          Where?

                    ASHLEY
          My butt.

Brandon shakes his head.

                    BRANDON
          You look great just the way you
          are.

                    ASHLEY
          Really?

                    BRANDON
          Yeah.

There is an awkward moment because Brandon has actually said
something nice to her and it makes her smile.

                    ASHLEY
          Thank you.

                    BRANDON
               (running from the moment)
          So did he tell you about the time
          we tried to cook Thanksgiving
          dinner?

                    ASHLEY
          No. But for some reason, he always
          sent my mother roses on
          Thanksgiving.

                    BRANDON
          Back when Vernon was sixteen and I
          was ten, we decided to give Moms
          the holiday off. Vernon had it all
          figured out.
                    (more)

                    BRANDON (cont'd)
Since we had just bought Moms this
used microwave oven for her
birthday, which she got pissed off
about and called it one more thing
to keep her in the kitchen, Vernon
figured we could watch the parade
that morning, go in the kitchen at
about two and have dinner on the
table by three and be out in the
street playing tackle football
before sundown. Plus Moms knew
letting us cook dinner would
develop some appreciation for her
services.

                    ASHLEY
Most men don't know what it takes
to cook Thanksgiving dinner.

                    BRANDON
We thought we knew. So the day
before, Vernon and I went to see
this brother who stole live
turkeys, gave 'em steroids and sold
'em in the projects. The turkey we
bought must've weighed fifty
pounds. Two o'clock, Thanksgiving
Day, we stroll into the kitchen to
start cooking the turkey. Vernon
says, first thing is bathe the bird
and grease him down with butter.
Cool, except we didn't have no
butter. So Vernon says we'll use
vegetable oil. He pours oil all
over the turkey and here we are
standing in the kitchen greasing
this big old bird down. We even
gave him a name. Cephus. We go to
put Cephus in the wave and he
started acting like he didn't wanna
fit. Vernon says put some more oil
on him and make him fit. We put
some more oil on him, shoved him in
and slammed the door shut. We set
the timer for one hour on high and
went outside to play.

                    ASHLEY
            (laughing)
No you didn't!

                    BRANDON
          Yes we did! And right in the
          middle of our game we heard this
          big explosion coming from our
          apartment, we all look up and out
          of the kitchen window comes Cephus
          flying through the air with the
          microwave door on his back. We all
          start running after Cephus like we
          were going out for a pass. Then
          the door drops off and hits this
          dude name Perry in the head.
          Vernon swore it stunted his growth
          'cause he ain't grown much since
          then. So we started callin' him
          Peanut.

                    ASHLEY
               (laughing harder)
          Stop!!

                    BRANDON
          I caught Cephus and all the fellas,
          thinking the game was still going
          on, tackled me. But he slipped out
          of my hands, from all that oil we
          put on him and went sliding down
          the street. We must have chased
          Cephus all around the projects for
          two hours. Needless to say, we ate
          McDonald's that Thanksgiving.
          Standing up, because we got our
          asses whipped good. True story, I
          swear.

                    ASHLEY
               (still laughing)
          I'm sure you guys learned your
          lesson.

                    BRANDON
          Yeah, whenever you go to cook a
          turkey, use butter instead of
          vegetable oil.

There is a moment of silence while Ashley settles down.

                    ASHLEY
          I'm gonna put on some music.

Brandon follows Ashley into the living room.

                         ASHLEY (cont'd)
              You know that story doesn't
              surprise me because he always had a
              clever way of doing things.

                         BRANDON
              But I was much better in school
              than he was. I was trying hard to
              get into college on a basketball
              scholarship.

                         ASHLEY
              What happened?

                         BRANDON
                   (stammers on the answer)
              I... I wasn't good enough. Prison
              was my college.

She hands him a stack of CDs.

                         BRANDON (cont'd)
              All my life I kept saying I'm not
              gonna be like my father.
                   (beat)
              Cats in the pen used to call me
              Little Henry Bell.

                         ASHLEY
              What was he in for?

The music comes on and it's a mid-tempo dance track. Ashley
starts dancing to the music.

                         BRANDON
              Being in the wrong place at the
              wrong time with the wrong crowd of
              people. I guess the apple don't
              fall too far from the tree. My
              father's father used to beat him
              and my father feels he has to keep
              the tradition going.

Brandon watches Ashley dancing.

                         BRANDON (cont'd)
              What the hell is that you're doing?

                         ASHLEY
              Oh, let me see your moves. Mr.
              know it all.

                    BRANDON
          You don't want me to get started!
          Now, I've got some moves.

Ashley turns up the music and moves the coffee table back.

                    ASHLEY
          Show me what cha' got!

Brandon starts slow and gradually gets into it. Ashley
laughs at him. Neither one are great dancers but they have
fun trying to show each other up.

The door bell RINGS. Ashley answers the door laughing.

                    TOM
          You guys having a party?

                    ASHLEY
          Yeah, come on in!

                    TOM
          Oh, no. I can't stay. I just came
          by to... I wanted to ask you... if
          you'd...
               (deep breath)
          ... like to have dinner some time.

Brandon is still dancing in the background.

                    BRANDON
          Hey, Tom, come on in and get some
          lessons!!

                    ASHLEY
               (gently)
          I don't think that would be a good
          idea. Thanks though.
               (beat)
          I'd still like to be friends.

Tom does a great job of hiding the rejection.

                    TOM
          Oh, okay.

He walks off. Ashley closes the door slowly.

BACK INSIDE

Ashley and Brandon continue dancing together. They aren't
saying any words but their body language says that they are
enjoying each other's company. Brandon starts to spoil the
moment by saying something but decides to just let the
feeling flow.

INT. VICTORIA'S APARTMENT - NIGHT

She sits down, picks up the phone and dials a number from a
piece of paper.

BRANDON AND ASHLEY DANCING

The phone RINGS and Ashley answers it. She hands the phone
to Brandon. He is surprised that he's gotten a call. She
turns the music down.

                    BRANDON
          Hello.

                                        INTER CUT WITH:

VICTORIA IN HER APARTMENT

                    VICTORIA
          Brandon...

                    BRANDON
          Hey, how'd you find me?

Brandon smiles and Ashley raises an eyebrow.

                    VICTORIA
          I begged your father for the
          number.

                    BRANDON
          So what's up? How are things on
          the home front?

                    VICTORIA
          Uh... Not too well.

                    BRANDON
          What's up?

                        VICTORIA
                    (careful)
                Well, your friend Peanut...
                    (takes a deep breath)
                ... was killed last night.

                        BRANDON
                    (hurt)
                DAMN!! What happened?

                        VICTORIA
                Some crack head took his cash, his
                jewelry and his gold tooth.

Brandon is quiet as his blood boils from within.

                        VICTORIA (cont'd)
                Brandon, are you there?

                        BRANDON
                Yeah.

                        VICTORIA
                Listen, call me as soon as you know
                when you're coming back so I can
                pick you up, okay?

                        BRANDON
                Somebody's gonna pay for this.

                        VICTORIA
                    (trying to cool him off)
                Brandon.

                        BRANDON
                Why don't you wire me money so I
                can come right home?

                        VICTORIA
                Just to kill some crack addict? I
                think not.

                        BRANDON
                    (justifying his hurt)
                I knew you wouldn't do it anyway.

Brandon slams the phone down. Ashley crosses over to
Brandon. She sees he is upset.

                        ASHLEY
                What's the matter, Brandon?

                    BRANDON
              (trying to play cool)
         Nothing. Nothing at all.

Ashley reaches out to stroke his shoulders but he gets up and
moves away from her. She knows he needs comforting but is
afraid of the anger building inside of him.

                    ASHLEY
         You can talk about it.

                    BRANDON
              (frustrated, confused
              and hurt)
         No... I can't...
              (the pain closes in on
              him)
         I can't talk anymore!!
              (raging)
         I WANNA DO SOMETHING!! But I don't
         know what! It's got to stop!!!
         It's got to stop!!

He slams his fist into the wall.

                    ASHLEY
              (remaining calm)
         I'm sure if you asked your parents--

                    BRANDON
              (angered)
         I'm not asking them!! We're not
         like you all are. We're not born
         with a bone in our body that allows
         us to easily forgive and forget.

                    ASHLEY
         I could give you some money.

                    BRANDON
         It's not just about me getting back
         home. Can't you see, it's
         happening everywhere! It's gonna
         catch up with me!

                    ASHLEY
         You're welcome to stay here.
              (she pauses)
         I'd like for you to stay. Just
         until the baby comes. You can get
         a job, save some money and help me
         around the house. But if you don't
         want to, it's okay.

Brandon is put on the spot to make a big decision. He
squirms because obviously he doesn't feel the same way he
felt before about her but he's not sure he wants to stay
longer.

                      BRANDON
                (short)
            I don't know.

He makes a fast exit into his bedroom.

EXT. SOUTH BAY CITY STREET - DAY

Brandon enters a restaurant that has a 'Dishwasher Wanted'
sign in the front window.

EXT. DRIVEWAY - DAY

The Jetta pulls in. Ashley sits in the car holding the
remote, trying to work up the courage to open the door. She
gives up, puts the remote away and goes in the house.

EXT. GRAVEYARD - DAY

Brandon stands over Vernon's grave amongst the Krutzer family
plots.

                      BRANDON
                (looking around)
            Damn, this place is hooked. I see
            why you wanted to be buried out
            here. These people have it better
            dead than most people have it
            living. I'll bet you're the only
            brother out here. Oh well, there
            goes the neighborhood.
                (beat)
            It ain't like they can pack up and
            leave.
                (beat)
            You know, I used to think that if
            we got out of the projects, we
            would have a better chance. But
            the shit is everywhere.

Brandon walks off.

EXT. OUTSIDE PAY PHONE - DAY

Across the street from the cemetery. Brandon drops a quarter
in the slot.

                    OPERATOR (O.S.)
          West Coast Telephone. May I help
          you?

                    BRANDON
          I wanna make a collect call to
          Panther from Brandon.

                                   INTER CUT WITH:

INT. PANTHER'S OFFICE - SAME

Panther picks up the phone.

                    PANTHER
          Yo, speak... Yeah, I'll accept the
          charges... Yo 'B', what's up? This
          ain't like you to call. What's got
          you stressin'?

                    BRANDON
          I'm okay. I just need to talk.

                    PANTHER
          You must've gotten the word on your
          boy. Listen, just chill out and
          remember what I used to rap to you
          in the joint about choices. You're
          still free to make your own
          choices. Right?

                    BRANDON
          Well, I've decided to stay out here
          longer. I've been too
          understanding with these people.

                    PANTHER
          I ain't advocating you go soft, but
          keep in mind that being
          understanding has its rewards, my
          brother.

INT. LIVING ROOM - LATE NIGHT

Brandon enters the front door. He stands in the middle of the dark living room, tensed, poised and ready for uncertain danger. Ashley enters in her night clothes on her way to the kitchen with some dirty dishes.

> ASHLEY
> Where have you been all day? Did
> you find a job?

He doesn't answer her.

> BRANDON
> I get the feeling you're not
> telling me everything.

> ASHLEY
> I'm not telling myself everything.
> It's not that easy. There are no
> clear cut answers.

> BRANDON
> That's bullshit. Maybe white
> people commit suicide for no
> reason.

> ASHLEY
> What do you want me to say? I
> mean, I know he was unhappy.

> BRANDON
> About what? What was upsetting
> him? Was it someone or something?
> What?

> ASHLEY
> I don't know. It could have been
> someone.

> BRANDON
> Who did he last see that I may not
> have talked to?

> ASHLEY
> He had been talking about wanting
> to go see one of his old Compton
> girlfriends.

Brandon is taken aback.

                    BRANDON
                 (to himself)
          She didn't tell me she talked to
          him recently. Let me borrow your
          car.

                    ASHLEY
          Where are you going?

                    BRANDON
          Compton.

                    ASHLEY
          You don't know how to drive a five
          speed.

                    BRANDON
          I can figure it out. Give me the
          keys.

                    ASHLEY
          You're not taking my new car, that
          you barely know how to drive, into
          Compton.

                    BRANDON
          Fuck it! I'll get there on my own.

Brandon barrels out of the house.

EXT. RESIDENTIAL STREETS - NIGHT

A montage of shots with Brandon walking the streets with his
thumb in the air. We hear the booming deep BASS of car
stereo woofers in the night.

A souped-up HYUNDAI SONATA with tinted windows comes down the
street and stops. The DRIVER turns down the rap music and
lowers the window.

                    DRIVER
          Where you headed, player?

                    BRANDON
          Compton.

                    DRIVER
          Dat's where I'm goin'. Jump in.

Brandon jumps in, the driver pumps the music up and peels
off.

INT. LIVING ROOM - SAME

Ashley stands in front of the TV holding one of the video
tapes Brandon made interviewing Vernon's friends. She is
pondering whether to put it in or not. She pops it in and
sits down on the floor in front of the TV.

EXT. FRONT OF MARY'S HOUSE - SAME

The Hyundai pulls up, and Brandon gets out. The house is
dark as Brandon walks up to the door and BANGS on it. A
light comes on and she lets him in.

INT. MARY'S LIVING ROOM - SAME

Brandon enters the front door.

                    MARY
               (half asleep)
          You lucky my man ain't over here or
          else your ass would be shot.

                    BRANDON
          How come you didn't tell me you
          talked to Vernon the other day?

                    MARY
          What the hell are you talking
          about? Oh, wait a second, yeah,
          yeah, I saw him.

                    BRANDON
          What did you talk about?

                    MARY
          I'm still asleep.

Brandon goes into her kitchen and starts ransacking her
cabinets.

                    MARY (cont'd)
          Boy, get out of my cabinets!!

                    BRANDON
          I'm gonna put some coffee on to
          wake your ass up.

                    MARY
          I ain't got no coffee!! Just wait
          a minute.

Brandon pauses.

                    MARY (cont'd)
          Okay, okay. Yeah, we ran into each
          other the other day.

                    BRANDON
          Where?

                    MARY
          What difference does it make?

                    BRANDON
               (losing control)
          WHERE!!!

                    MARY
          Here! He came over here one night.
          Okay?

                    BRANDON
          You told me you hadn't seen him in
          years.

                    MARY
          I didn't wanna remember him that
          way. That wasn't the Vernon I was
          in love with.
               (she pauses a moment
               and sits down)
          I stuck with him when he was
          nobody. I helped him through law
          school. All she did was marry him.
          She got the house in PV Hills and
          the papers on him. When he walked
          out on me, I cried... He was the
          best man that I've ever had.

                    BRANDON
          I don't understand why he dumped
          you for Ashley.

                    MARY
          Maybe I just didn't fit with the
          corporate world he was about to
          enter. I always figured he'd
          eventually come back but not like
          that. Not like the other night.
          He said Ashley was out of town so
          we could fool around just like old
          times. But it wasn't.
               (more)

                         MARY (cont'd)
          I kissed him once and he started
          rattling off all this crazy
          philosophical bullshit.

                         BRANDON
          Like...?

                         MARY
          About how much he loved Ashley but
          there was a side of him that he
          could never share with her and he
          was afraid of it. He was saying
          all this while he had his arms
          around me.

                         BRANDON
          What did you say to him?

                         MARY
          I cut him short, told him he was
          fucking crazy and that bitch had
          locked up his mind. I told him he
          may as well be dead.
               (beat)
          I wasn't the one who made him flip
          though. He was already gone.
               (bows her head in shame)
          I coulda taken good care of him.
          But he didn't want me to. I even
          sent all of his letters back to
          him.

Brandon jumps to attention.

                         BRANDON
          When did you send them?

                         MARY
          A few days after he came over.

Mary comes back to reality.

                         MARY (cont'd)
          I don't know why you're over here
          screaming at me. You need to go
          get in Ashley's face.

Thinking about the letters, Brandon exits.

INT. ASHLEY'S HOUSE - NIGHT

Ashley now has the whole box of tapes spread out all over the
floor. She is glued to the TV. On the TV:

                    FIFTH FRIEND
          Most things that make normal men
          happy, wasn't working for Vernon.
          A nice house, good job, beautiful
          wife. What more could a man have
          asked for? Born white I guess.
          I'm thankful.

EXT. DESOLATE STREET - NIGHT

Brandon walking down the street trying to hitch a ride back
to Palos Verdes.

He sees an RTD bus coming down the street and runs to the bus
stop. The bus stops and lets him on.

INT. ASHLEY'S HOUSE - NIGHT

CLOSE ON TV SCREEN. All we see is static. The tape has
stopped. Ashley is still sitting on the floor in front of
the TV. She wipes the tears away from her eyes. Ashley
hears car tires screeching in the street and speeding off.
She hears Carol screaming from outside.

                    CAROL (O.S.)
               (screaming)
          YOU CRAZY SON OF A BITCH!!!

The doorbell RINGS. Ashley opens the door and sees Carol
standing on the porch dressed from a date and staggering.
She tries not to let on that she's had too much to drink.

                    CAROL (cont'd)
               (sweet as pie)
          Hi, Ashley, honey. Sorry to bother
          you, but--
               (she burps)
          Um, excuse me. But I... I'm sure
          you heard him drive off... I just
          got ditched... I need a place to
          stay.

                    ASHLEY
          Sure, come on in.

                    CAROL
               (staggers in)
          I tell you, you just can't control
          them. You know... them.

                         ASHLEY
              I know. Men are pigs.

                         CAROL
                    (wasted)
              Not all men, Ashley. Black men,
              Ashley. Okay, so he's supposed to
              be totally taking me... to a
              concert at the Strand and some soul
              sister starts making goo-goo eyes
              at him. I knew if I went to the
              bathroom he was gonna go over
              there. So I pretended to go and
              sure enough he went over to her
              table. They're dogs, Ashley. Oh,
              Ashley, I don't have to tell you.
              You used to be married to one. I
              told him to take me home!! Or take
              me to my friend's house.
                    (beat)
              Can I use your bathroom? I've got
              to pee.

She continues babbling as she slowly makes her way to the
bathroom.

                         ASHLEY
              Sure.

                         CAROL
              They think they want to go out with
              us. They're just looking for a
              good time until something better
              comes along. Vernon was the same
              way.

                         ASHLEY
              I don't think so.

                         CAROL
              He may have married you but he
              still liked his brown sugar. I'll
              bet he had some stashed away
              somewhere.

                         ASHLEY
                    (refusing to believe her)
              You've got Vernon mixed up with
              someone else.

Carol disappears into the bathroom and leaves Ashley to
ponder her last words.

BRANDON ENTERS THE FRONT DOOR

and goes straight to his room.

IN HIS ROOM

He locates a stack of mail buried under a pile of clothes.
He finds the envelope from Mary with all the letters.

Brandon comes out of his room and

INTO THE LIVING ROOM

He hands Ashley a stack of mail and continues reading the
letters.

                    ASHLEY
               (still pre-occupied)
          Your--your mother called. You can
          call her back.

                    BRANDON
          Thanks, but no thanks.

                    ASHLEY
               (reprimanding)
          Why not? She's your mother.

                    BRANDON
               (blows up at her)
          BECAUSE I DON'T WANT TO!!!
               (anger mixed with hurt)
          Ain't nothing she can do without my
          old man's word. I ain't begging
          him for shit and that's what he
          wants.
               (calmer)
          That's why.

Brandon goes to the kitchen and gets a bottle of water out of
the refrigerator and chugs it.

                    ASHLEY
          I watched your tapes.

                    BRANDON
          I hope you learned something.

                    ASHLEY
As a matter of fact, I did. Vernon
was unhappy with--

                    CAROL(O.S.)
  Ashley!

Carol comes staggering out of the bathroom.

                    CAROL (cont'd)
Ashley, may I have some water?

Carol moves toward the kitchen and comes face-to-face with
Brandon. They stare at each other.

                    CAROL (cont'd)
It's the Boogeyman.

Ashley grabs a bottle of water out of the refrigerator and
then puts her arm around Carol and walks her toward the
bedroom.

                    ASHLEY
You're sleeping in my bed tonight.

                    CAROL
No, I'm staying up. Somebody has
to protect you from Shaft.

Ashley puts Carol to bed and closes the door. She returns to
the living room to see Brandon picking up the tapes off the
floor.

                    ASHLEY
Vernon did not want to be who he
was. He was trying to run from
something he couldn't escape. The
pressure got too great so he had to
get out.

                    BRANDON
What kind of fucked up analysis is
that?

                    ASHLEY
He was trying to stay in touch with
himself, but... but he felt more
comfortable around whites. He was
questioning his blackness.

                    BRANDON
      (looks at her like she's
      crazy)
           (more)

                        BRANDON (cont'd)
          And where did you get this from?
          Listening to Public Enemy? What
          would happen if you saw a Spike Lee
          film? Then you could predict all
          of us.
                  (very sarcastic)
          They could reinstate slavery
          because Ashley knows all about and
          how to control niggers.
                  (back to reality)
          I'm going to bed.

He walks away. She is furious and picks up one of his rolled
up newspapers and throws it at him, barely missing his head.

He charges across the room and snatches her by her wrist.
She takes a swing at him with her free hand and he grabs her
other wrist as she struggles to break free.

                        BRANDON (cont'd)
          What the hell's wrong with you?

                        ASHLEY
          You won't listen to me!!!

Brandon releases her by pushing her down on the couch.

                        BRANDON
          Because you don't know what the
          hell is going on!!

                        ASHLEY
                  (breaks down)
          I KNOW I DON'T! BUT AT LEAST I'M
          TRYING!! And I was trying to find
          out what was going on with Vernon!!
                  (crying)
          Now I have all of these thoughts in
          my head and they're dying to come
          out and I have no one to tell them
          to! And you've been on my back
          screaming, 'Talk to me!', 'Give me
          some answers!' and now you won't
          even listen to what I have to say!!

Ashley collects herself before going on.

                        ASHLEY cont'd)
          I'm... I'm trying to tell you why
          your brother, my husband, didn't
          want to live anymore.

Brandon gives Ashley his attention.

> ASHLEY
> He wanted to wait to get married so
> his baby brother could be best man.
> But when you told him you wouldn't
> because you did not approve of the
> marriage...you broke his heart.

This information weakens Brandon and he has to sit down. He
tries to dismiss the notion.

> BRANDON
> Bullshit!

> ASHLEY
> He didn't stop loving you because
> you were a convict. Why did you
> have to stop loving him?

> BRANDON
> (very defensive)
> I never said I didn't love him!!

> ASHLEY
> Your coming out here has helped me
> to understand a lot of things for
> myself. But you didn't have to
> come out to find out why Vernon
> killed himself. You knew all
> along.

Brandon is breathing heavily trying to hold back the tears.

> BRANDON
> (ashamed and still trying
>   to defend himself)
> That's no reason for anyone to
> shoot themselves.

> ASHLEY
> If I had to choose between my
> family, friends and him I'd do the
> same thing.

Brandon covers his face and cries softly. Ashley sits beside
him and rubs his back.

> ASHLEY (cont'd)
> (comforting)
> You know, I think Vernon was just
> trying to make everybody happy. I
> tried to tell him not to worry
> about what people think.

Brandon moves away from her.

                    BRANDON
          Have you ever been crossing the
          street and seen people reach over
          and lock their car doors? Have you
          ever been followed through a store
          by a security guard? You better
          hope your kid comes out light
          enough to pass for white.

                    ASHLEY
          But I won't let my child use color
          as an excuse.

Brandon chuckles more to himself than at her comment.

                    BRANDON
          I lied. I was very good at
          basketball. I even got my
          scholarship. But one night, Deebo,
          the local drug dealer, was hanging
          out with me and the fellas. He was
          giving them all free hits of crack
          trying to get them hooked. You
          know, make 'em future customers.
          He knew I used to run a little pot
          on the side so he thought for sure
          I'd be down. Well I wasn't, so he
          started calling me a wimp.
               (reliving the night in his
               mind)
          So I got up to walk away and he
          threw a bottle and hit me in the
          back of the head. I shouldn't have
          stopped.

                    ASHLEY
               (agreeing and wishing his
               fate were different)
          You should have just kept walking.

                    BRANDON
          But I tried to fight him. As soon
          as I got the best of him, he
          whipped out a knife and stabbed me
          in the arm.

Ashley winces.

                    BRANDON (cont'd)
               (oblivious to her
               presence)
                    (more)

                    BRANDON (cont'd)
          All of a sudden I leaped off the
          ground like Superman, grabbed him
          with one hand and started throwing
          him all over the place.

Brandon is telling the story but reenacting the emotion of
the incident.

                    BRANDON (cont'd)
          I bashed his head up against the
          wall so hard so many times that
          blood was splattering all over
          everybody's clothes and I kept
          screaming "I HATE YOU, MOTHER
          FUCKER, I HATE YOU!"

Brandon settles down, returning to the present.

                    BRANDON (cont'd)
          I didn't remember any of it, until
          I started having nightmares in
          prison. I was a hero for a while
          because I killed a drug dealer. I
          didn't wanna be that kind of hero.
          If I had been born left handed,
          like Vernon, I would have been all
          right. But I wasn't and I got
          twenty years with parole in five.
          That's my excuse.

                    ASHLEY
          But you got through it.

Brandon knows that she is referring to Vernon.

                    BRANDON
          I guess he wasn't as perfect as we
          wanted him to be.

                    ASHLEY
          He was pretty close. So what are
          we gonna do?

                    BRANDON
               (after a moment of thought
               and then with a subtle
               new attitude)
          Maybe I did need to come out here.
          Maybe I needed to find out why I've
          been trying to kill myself.
               (Brandon looks up at her)
          Let's keep going.

They give each other a hug for strength and support.

EXT. MONTAGE OF SHOTS - DAY

Of the ocean, the waves, the beach and the mountains.

A MONTAGE OF SHOTS WITH BRANDON

getting off the bus and entering his restaurant job.

Washing dishes at work.

Going to the bank with his check.

EXT. BEACH - DAY

Brandon is sitting on the sand. He is writing in his notepad.

> BRANDON (V.O.)
> Panther, I've been trying to write
> this piece but I can't seem to
> decide on what it is I want to say.
> Maybe it's because now I wanna say
> so much I don't know where to
> begin.

INT. LIVING ROOM - DAY

Brandon cleaning up the house.

In the kitchen trying to cook.

Brandon reaches out his hand to a chair and the hand receives
his. He slowly lifts a very pregnant Ashley up and helps her
to the kitchen table to a meal he has cooked. She sits down
and takes a bite and the look on her face lets us know it's
terrible.

Ashley trying to teach Brandon how to drive her five speed.
The car is bucking back and forth like a wild horse.

Brandon trying to shoot basketball with his left hand.

Brandon mailing a letter.

Ashley tasting something Brandon is trying to cook. She
gives a 'better' nod.

Another driving lesson.

A pregnant Ashley dragging Brandon out of bed in the middle of the night.

The car backing out of the driveway.

Ashley in the living room fidgeting nervously with a spoon.

The car pulls up in the driveway.

Brandon enters the front door and hands her a bag and goes back to bed. She opens the bag and digs right into a pint of ice cream.

Brandon in the kitchen making a royal mess.

Brandon entering Ashley's bedroom and waking her up with a cake that says 'Happy Birthday Ashley and Brandon.' They exchange gifts.

Brandon re-enters the bedroom modeling a pair of short pants. She applauds. She opens her present and it's a blue and red Atlanta Braves baseball hat. She puts it on. She then presents him with a new Word Processor.

Brandon taking the recycle bins to the recycle center.

Brandon on the beach writing.

Brandon mailing the letter.

INT. BELL LIVING ROOM - DAY

Clarice opens a letter from Brandon and reads it.

>   BRANDON (V.O.)
>   "Dear Mom. I'm just writing to say
>   I'm doing well. I almost have
>   enough money saved up to get back
>   to Atlanta. Please don't tell Pops
>   I'm coming back because I want to
>   try and get a place of my own.
>   Ashley is doing great. She is as
>   big as a house and the baby should
>   be here any day."

Clarice lowers the letter. She thinks a moment about the baby line. She reads on.

INT. BRANDON'S ROOM - DAY

Brandon is writing. Ashley appears in the doorway holding her
back with a look of pain on her face. He looks at her and
knows it's time. He jumps up off the bed. Brandon runs
around the house frantic before he remembers what he's
supposed to do to get her to the hospital.

EXT. CITY STREETS - DAY

The Jetta speeds along. Brandon drives into the hospital
parking lot.

INT. HOSPITAL WAITING ROOM - DAY

Brandon pacing back and forth with his camcorder hanging off
his shoulder. The SECOND DOCTOR comes out of the operating
room removing his mask.

                    SECOND DOCTOR
               Congratulations, it's a boy.
               You're an Uncle.

Brandon takes a moment to let it all sink in.

                    BRANDON
          I'm a... I'm a... an uncle?

                    SECOND DOCTOR
               Yes.

Brandon jumps up and down, does bell kicks and takes off
running into the delivery room.

The Doctor chases after him.

                    SECOND DOCTOR (cont'd)
               Wait, you can't go in there yet!

EXT. DRIVEWAY - DAY

Brandon pulls into the driveway, gets out of the driver's
side with the camcorder on record. He runs around to open
the door for Ashley. She gets out with the baby as he
videotapes the event.

INT. LIVING ROOM - MOMENTS LATER

Ashley sits down on the couch and plays with the baby while
Brandon sets the camcorder up on the tripod.

> BRANDON
> (from behind the camera)
> Okay, I'm ready.

> ASHLEY
> (to the baby)
> Say hi to Grandma and Grandpa.
> Vernon Jr., say hi to your
> grandparents.

A CLOSE SHOT OF ASHLEY HOLDING THE BABY

on the TV screen. The CAMERA pulls back slowly to reveal
Clarice and Henry in their living room watching the video
tape with an open Federal Express package on the coffee
table. They are in a trance watching the mother and child.

EXT. ASHLEY'S HOUSE - DAY

The Jetta is in the driveway.

INT. BRANDON'S CONCENTRATED FACE - DAY

He is teaching himself how to put on a diaper by practicing
on a baby doll. The phone RINGS. He hides the doll under
the couch and answers the phone.

> BRANDON
> Hello.

> OPERATOR (O.S.)
> I have a collect call from Mr.
> Henry Bell. Will you accept the
> charges?

> BRANDON
> Yeah.

> INTER CUT WITH:

INT. LIVING ROOM - SAME

Henry on the phone.

                    HENRY
          Brandon. This is your old man.

An awkward moment of silence from both parties.

                    HENRY (cont'd)
          We, uh, we got the tapes.

                    BRANDON
          Did you watch them?

                    HENRY
          Yeah, we did. Uh, the baby looks
          healthy. How much did he weigh?

                    BRANDON
          Six pounds, six ounces.

                    HENRY
          Good, good.

Another awkward moment of silence. Ashley enters carrying
the baby.

                    BRANDON
          You know, Dad, I'm glad you called.
          Vernon quit. He gave up. Let's
          not you and I give up.

                    HENRY
               (hiding his feelings)
          Your mother made me call.

                    BRANDON
          Yo, Pops, it's okay, chill out.

                    HENRY
          How's the baby's mother doing?

                    BRANDON
          Here, I'll let you ask her.

He hands the phone to Ashley. Brandon takes the baby.

                    ASHLEY
          Hello.

                    HENRY
          Hello. How's the baby?

                    ASHLEY
          He's fine. He looks just like his
          Daddy.

                    HENRY
               (chuckles)
          He looks just like his Granddad.
               (beat)
          You hanging in there?

                    ASHLEY
          I'm doing fine. Brandon has been
          taking great care of me. I'm going
          to miss having him around.

                    HENRY
               (awkward, but trying)
          If there's anything you need, you
          let us know. We don't have much
          but we'll try and do what we can.

                    ASHLEY
          Thanks, Mr. Bell.

                    HENRY
          Oh, call me Henry.

Touched by his openness, Ashley wipes a tear from her eye.

                    ASHLEY
          Thank you, Henry.

                    HENRY
          And take good care of my Grandson.

                    ASHLEY
               (sniffles)
          I will. Bye now.

She gives the phone to Brandon and she dashes into the
bedroom.

                    BRANDON
          Let me speak to Mama.

Henry gives the phone to Clarice.

                    CLARICE
               (joyous)
          Hi, Son. You did a good job
          delivering a beautiful baby.

                    BRANDON
          Ah, I didn't do anything. The
          Doctor did all the work. I had to
          be carried out of the delivery
          room.
               (more)

                    BRANDON (cont'd)
               (beat)
          I fainted.

                    CLARICE
          Your Daddy has watched this tape at
          least ten times. He is so proud.
          The first few times he kept going
          "re-wind it, play it again. Look
          at his eyes, they look like mine.
          Back it up."
               (beat)
          You can come on home now.

                    BRANDON
          I'll be there tomorrow afternoon.
          Just in time for my progress report
          with my parole officer. And my drug
          test.

                    CLARICE
          I'll see you when you get here.

                    BRANDON
          Bye now.

Brandon hangs up. He picks up the phone and makes another
call. Victoria's answering machine picks up.

                    VICTORIA (O.S.)
          I'm not in right now, leave a
          message and I'll call you back.

                    BRANDON
          Hi, it's me. I was just calling to
          apologize for not staying in touch.
          I'm going to be home soon and I'd
          like to see you. If you'll accept
          my apology.

He hangs up and hears Ashley crying in her bedroom. He goes
into

ASHLEY'S BEDROOM

and she is sprawled out on the bed bawling her eyes out.
Brandon lifts her up, hugs her and lets her cry on his
shoulder.

                    ASHLEY
               (through her tears)
          Why couldn't he have accepted me
          earlier?! Why?
               (more)

                    ASHLEY (cont'd)
          He'd still have a son, I'd still
          have a husband. My baby would have
          a father!!!

Brandon hugs her tighter as she cries loudly and
uncontrollably.

                    BRANDON
          Some people take a while to accept
          things. You get the award for
          being the most resilient. Don't
          stop now, okay?

She shakes her head.

                    BRANDON (cont'd)
          You still have a long journey ahead
          of you.

Ashley throws her arms around Brandon and hugs and squeezes
him tight.

                    ASHLEY
               (very sad)
          Please don't go! I was just
          starting to not dislike you.

Brandon smiles.

EXT. FRONT OF THE HOUSE - DAY

Brandon comes out of the house struggling with several
suitcases and his duffle bag. He makes his way across the
yard and down to the sidewalk. He looks at all of his
luggage.

                    BRANDON
          I don't remember bringing this much
          shit.

Tom comes walking down the street with a big gift for the
baby.

                    BRANDON (cont'd)
          Tom, what's up, my brother?

                    TOM
          Hello, Brandon. I forgot you were
          leaving today. You need a ride to
          the airport?

                         BRANDON
          Thanks but I've got a cab on the
          way. What ya got?

                         TOM
                   (excited)
          I bought a little red scooter for
          the baby.

                         BRANDON
          What is he going to do with a
          scooter?

                         TOM
          Ride it?

                         BRANDON
          Tom, he's not even crawling yet.
          He can't even sit up on his own.
          He can barely hit his diaper when
          he goes to the bathroom and it's
          taped to his butt. What in the
          hell did you buy him a scooter for?

                         TOM
          Maybe he can grow into it.

                         BRANDON
          You are one of a kind. Ashley's
          inside, why don't you take it in to
          her so she can give you the same
          lecture.

                         TOM
          Oh, okay.

Tom goes inside. The cab pulls up and the Driver gets out.

                         CABBIE
          Boy, you've got a few pieces.
          Where you headed?

                         BRANDON
          Back to Atlanta.

                         CABBIE
          Ah, how 'bout them Braves? I heard
          there's some good living out there.

                         BRANDON
          I miss Atlanta. But there's good
          living everywhere. It's what you
          make of it.

                    CABBIE
        But the houses are cheaper.

                    BRANDON
        Yeah, but you don't have the beach
        and the mountains within minutes.

                    CABBIE
        I guess you could look at it that
        way.

                    BRANDON
        Yeap.

Tom comes out of the house.

                    TOM
        Brandon, you have a safe trip.

                    BRANDON
        Look here, I want you to look out
        for Ashley when I leave.

                    TOM
        Oh, I will.

                    BRANDON
            (in his face)
        I know you want to but if I find
        out you're just coming around
        because she was down with a
        brother... I swear... I'll walk
        back to California and beat the
        shit out of you.

                    TOM
        Don't worry, Brandon, I promise
        I'll take care of her.

Brandon shakes his hand and slaps him on the shoulder.

                    BRANDON
        Peace.

Tom heads back up the street. Brandon starts toward the
house.

                    BRANDON (cont'd)
            (to the Cabbie)
        I'll be right with you.

Brandon stops when he hears the latch on the garage door
rattle.

The CAMERA moves in slowly as the garage door raises up and
Ashley is standing in the garage. She comes out and they
meet on the front lawn. He gives her a congratulatory hug
for tackling her fear of the garage. They are both at a loss
for words.

                    ASHLEY
          Be careful. Have a safe trip and
          all that other good stuff. Thanks
          for taking care of me.

                    BRANDON
          No, thanks for taking care of me.
          I'm gonna try and come back out for
          Christmas. Maybe I'll have my
          portfolio by then and I can sell it
          for a plane ticket. If they don't
          make me go back to prison.

                    ASHLEY
          They won't. I'll write the parole
          board a letter saying you've been
          on good behavior.

                    BRANDON
          Thanks.

                    ASHLEY
          Well, semi-good behavior. He still
          needs to work on his language.

                    BRANDON
          I haven't said one bad word since
          the baby came home. I'm gonna send
          you some money when I get back to
          Atlanta.

                    ASHLEY
          You don't have to do that, really.
          We're gonna be okay.

                    BRANDON
          What if I send some things for the
          baby? Like toys and clothes. Some
          hooded sweat shirts.

                    ASHLEY
               (laughs)
          Yeah, that'll work.

Brandon gives her one last hug and turns and gets in the cab.
The cab drives off.

INT. BACK OF THE CAB - DAY

A medium shot of Brandon thinking as the cab drives down the
Palos Verdes mountain.

>   BRANDON (V.O.)
>   I can't believe it's been almost a
>   year and I haven't gotten this
>   piece written. I still don't have
>   all the answers, but I do have some
>   understanding. It has a lot to do
>   with us accepting and respecting
>   ourselves for who we are and not
>   trying to live up to anyone else's
>   expectations; good or bad. Or
>   trying to run from or over-express
>   who we are. We just need to be
>   content with ourselves first and
>   stay black. I may not have a
>   finished article, but I do have
>   hope for the future. Peace!

>   DISSOLVE TO:

A LONG CRANE SHOT

as the cab continues down the mountainside.

>   FADE OUT:

(CREDITS ROLL)

Scripts written by Gregory LeGrand Kerns and developed by Unique Tree Films from 1991-1999:

The Radical View

Devil 101 (original story by Geoffrey H. Miller)

Every Time We Meet (original story by Geoffrey H. Miller)

Big Day at the Kirklands

3 Girlfriends & A Wife

Mr. Sandman

Country Club Clowns

GK's Comedy House

Michael's Magical Toy Box

See Sally Run

Weekend In New England

Soul Night

Tony's Camcorder

That Buckhead Girl

Feature films produced by Unique Tree Films:

The Good-Bye Tape

Additional works by Gregory LeGrand Kerns

Screenplays:

Henry's Big Problem

Brother Without A Cause

That Guy At Work

Atlanta Nights

The Opposite Killers

Stage plays:

Mama's Little Boys

The Doughnut Shop

Television pilots:

What R U Waiting 4

Nights in Newport Beach

Produced short films:

Grown Folks Talkin'

Pimp Tales

Novel:

Black in Orange County

Geoff Miller and I proudly displaying the boxes we made by hand to promote Michael's Magical Toybox. June 1994.

The toy boxes finished and ready to send to studio executives. A few of the executives asked if they could keep the box. Of course we said yes.

UNIQUE TREE FILMS PRESENTS

THE GOOD-BYE TAPE

Sometimes it's hard to let go.

UNIQUE TREE FILMS PRESENTS "THE GOOD-BYE TAPE"
STARRING CHARLES ALLEN GREGORY LEGRAND KERNS
J.W. MYERS LYN ROSS REGINA RYER AND VIDA VASAITIS
MUSIC BY MICHAEL LEWIS FEATURING SONGS BY SPORTIN' HARD
EDITOR HARVEY LANDY DIRECTORS OF PHOTOGRAPHY
JEFF NICHOLSON MICHAEL J. SCHERLIS AND SPECNER THORNTON
EXECUTIVE PRODUCER JEFF NICHOLSON PRODUCER GEOFFREY H. MILLER
WRITTEN, PRODUCED AND DIRECTED BY GREGORY LEGRAND KERNS

© 1995 UNIQUE TREE FILMS

*In 1994, Geoff and I produced the feature The Good-Bye Tape. From
The Radical View, we cast Regina (far right) and Charles (second from
right) in the movie.*

ABOUT THE WRITER

GREGORY LEGRAND KERNS

Long before he had the idea for *The Radical View*, Mr. Kerns was a drama major at the prestigious University of North Carolina School of the Arts, alongside Peter Hedges (*Dan in Real Life*), Mary Louise Parker (*Weeds*) and Joe Mantello (*Wicked*). In college, Mr. Kerns began writing sketch comedy shows and one-act plays. In 1988, his first full-length play, *Mama's Little Boys*, was produced at the National Black Theatre in Harlem. A few years later, he made the move to Hollywood and wrote *The Radical View*.

In 1995, Mr. Kerns wrote, co-produced, directed and starred in a feature-length video entitled *The Good-Bye Tape*. The following year he directed *Jack Fell Down*, a 30-minute film featuring *ET*'s Dee Wallace Stone. In 2004, Mr. Kerns collaborated with Spike Lee's *Get on the Bus* editor Leander Sales to produce the comedy *Grown Folks Talkin'*.

As a writer and producer, Mr. Kerns has worked on television shows for the Disney Channel, MTV and BET. In addition to his writing background, Mr. Kerns has more than 20 years of hands-on film and video production experience. He has shared his creative talent with companies such as Microsoft, Ingram Micro, Cisco Systems, BP, BMW, AT&T and Verizon Wireless. Currently, Mr. Kerns is an associate creative director at G2 Direct & Digital in New York City.

Mr. Kerns lives in New Jersey and is married to his college sweetheart, Deneen Graham-Kerns.

www.ingramcontent.com/pod-product-compliance
Lightning Source LLC
Chambersburg PA
CBHW071353170626
46811CB00003B/1117